The Motor Boat Club and The Wireless

by H. Irving Hancock

CHAPTER I

A SPARK PUTS THREE BOYS AND A BOAT ON THE JUMP

"Ho, ho, ho—hum!" grumbled Hank Butts, vainly trying to stifle a prodigious yawn. "This may be what Mr. Seaton calls a vacation on full pay, but I'd rather work."

"It *is* fearfully dull, loafing around, in this fashion, on a lonely island, yet in plain sight of the sea that we long to rove over," nodded Captain Tom Halstead of the motor yacht "Restless."

"Yet Hank just put us in mind of the fact that we're getting paid for our time," laughed Joe Dawson, the least restless of the trio of young Motor Boat Club boys.

"Oh it's all right on the pay end," agreed Hank, readily. "But just think of a young fellow, full of life and hope, with a dozen ambitions and a hustling nature, taking up with a job of this kind!"

"What kind of job?" inquired Captain Tom.

"The job of being bored," answered Butts, solemnly. "I could have had that kind of job back on Long Island."

"Without the pay," amended Joe Dawson, with another quiet smile.

"But ten days of being bored *does* grow rather wearisome, even with the pay for a solace," agreed Tom Halstead.

Ting-ling-ling! The soft jangling of a bell from one of the rooms of the seashore bungalow, on the porch of which the boys sat, broke in on them.

"Hurrah, Joe! Hustle and get that message," begged Hank, almost sitting up straight in the porch chair, with a comical pretense of excitement. "It's sure to be from Mr. Seaton this time."

"Likely," grinned Joe, as he rose and crossed the porch in leisurely fashion. The jangling of the bell continued. The bell was a rather clumsy, yet sufficing device that young Dawson had attached to the wireless telegraph apparatus.

For, though this bungalow on a little island southwest of Beaufort, North Carolina, had an appearance of being wholly out of the world, yet the absent owner, Mr. Powell Seaton, had contrived to put his place very much "in the world" by installing wireless telegraphy at the bungalow. On the premises was operated a complete electrical plant that furnished energy enough to send messages for hundreds of miles along the coast.

For Joe, the mechanical genius of the Motor Boat Club, had always had a passion for telegraphy. Of late he had gone in in earnest for the wireless kind, and had rapidly mastered its most essential details.

The bell told when electrical waves were rushing through the air at marvelous speed, though it did not distinguish between any general wave and the special call for this bungalow station, which was by the letters "CBA."

3

When Joe Dawson went into the room under the tall aerials that hung from the mast, he expected to listen only to some message not in the least intended for this station.

Seating himself by the relay, with its Morse register close at hand, Joe Dawson picked up and adjusted the head-band with its pair of watch-case receivers. He then hastily picked up a pencil, shoved a pad of paper close under his hand and listened.

All this he did with a dull, listless air. He had not the slightest forewarning of the great jolt that was soon to come to himself and his comrades out of the atmosphere.

The call, whatever it was, had ended. Yet, after a pause of a few seconds, it began to sound again. Joe's listless air vanished as the new set of dots and dashes came in, clamoring in clicking haste against his ear drums.

"To Every Wireless Station—Urgent!" ran the first few words. Joe's nimble fingers pushed his pencil, recording letter after letter until these words were down. Then, dropping his pencil for the sending key, young Dawson transmitted a crashing electric impulse into the air, flashing through space over hundreds of miles the station signal, "CBA."

"Have you a fast, seaworthy boat within immediate call?" came back out of the invisible distance over the ocean.

"A twenty-six-mile sea-going motor boat right at the pier here," Joe flashed back, again adding his signature, "CBA."

"Good!" came back the answer. "Then listen hard—act quick—life at stake!"

Joe Dawson not only listened. His thoughts flew with the dots and dashes of the wireless message; his right hand rushed the pencil in recording all of that wonderful message as it came to him. It was tragedy that Dawson wrote down at the dictation of this impatient operator far out on the Atlantic highways. Almost in the midst of it came a feverish break-in from land, and another hand was playing in the great game of life and death, fame and dishonor, riches and intrigue. All was being unfolded by means of the unseen, far-reaching wireless telegraph.

As Joe listened, wrote, and occasionally broke in to send a few words, the dew of cold perspiration stood out on his brow. His fingers trembled. With a great effort of the will this motor boat boy steadied his nerves and muscles in order to see through to the end this mysterious thing coming out of space.

While this was going on, Joe Dawson did not call out to either of his comrades. With an instinct that worked as fast as the wireless messages themselves, young Dawson chose to put off calling the other motor boat boys until he had the whole startling tale to tell them—until he had in complete form the coming orders that would send all three of them and the "Restless" on a tireless sea-chase.

While this flood of dots and dashes is coming in from seaward, and from landward, it is well that the reader be put in possession of some information that will make clearer to him the nature of the dramatic events that followed this sudden in-pouring of wireless messages to the little "CBA" bungalow station on this island off the North Carolina coast.

4

Readers of the preceding volume of this series, "THE MOTOR BOAT CLUB OFF LONG ISLAND," will at once recall that story, throbbing with the interest of human life—will remember how faithfully and wisely Tom Halstead, Joe Dawson and Hank Butts, all members of the Motor Boat Club, served that leader in Wall Street finance, Francis Delavan, and the latter's nervous, wavering friend, Eben Moddridge. To such former readers the tale is familiar of how the Motor Boat Club boys aided materially in frustrating a great conspiracy in finance, aimed against their employer. Saved from ruin by the grit, keenness and loyalty of these three members of the Motor Boat Club, Messrs. Delavan and Moddridge had handsomely rewarded the boys for their signal services.

As Hank Butts preferred, for family reasons, to spend his summers, and much of his other time, on Long Island, he had been presented with a thirty-foot launch, a shore lot at East Hampton, and a "shack" and pier. Tom Halstead and Joe Dawson, fast friends and both from the same little Kennebec River village, preferring always the broad ocean, had been made the owners of the "Soudan," a fine, sea-going, fifty-five foot motor cruising yacht built for deep sea work. Though the "Soudan" had a very comfortable beam of fifteen feet, she was nevertheless equipped with twin gasoline motors that could send her over the waters at some twenty-five or twenty-six miles an hour.

With the gift of the boat to Tom and Joe came also a present of money enough to make the two new young owners able to put her in commission and keep her going for awhile.

It was not intended by Messrs. Delavan and Moddridge that Tom Halstead and Joe Dawson should be able to keep their new prize and property running for their own pleasure. On the contrary the givers of this splendid present believed that the two boys would ply under charter for wealthy pleasure seekers, thus making a splendid living. In summer there were the northern waters; in winter the southern waters. Thus it was believed that Captain Tom Halstead and Engineer Joe Dawson would be in a position to earn a handsome income from their boat the year around. At any time, should they so choose, they could sell the boat.

Sell her? It would almost have broken honest, impulsive, loyal Tom Halstead's heart to sell this precious boat! Joe Dawson, quiet though he was, would have flown into a rage at any suggestion of his parting with his interest in the handsome, capable little craft!

The owners had re-christened the boat the "Restless." Within ten days after the boys had left the employ of Mr. Delavan, Captain Tom had encountered Mr. Powell Seaton in New York. A few hours after that meeting the boys had had their boat chartered for at least the month of September. Then, after receiving their orders, they proceeded south to their present location on Lonely Island, five miles off the mainland. They were accompanied by Hank Butts, who had left his small boat in other hands and accepted temporary employment on the "Restless."

The island possessed an area of about half a square mile. The bungalow itself, a shed that was used as an electric power station, and a third building that

5

contained a telescope and some other astronomical apparatus were the sole interesting features of this island.

After the chartering, and the payment of half the hire-money in advance for the month, not one of these Motor Boat Club boys had laid eyes on Mr. Powell Seaton. After cruising down from New York, and taking possession of the bungalow, as ordered, they had remained there ten whole days, idle and wondering. Idle, that is, except for running the electric power plant as much as was needed, making their own beds and doing their own cooking.

For what purpose had Powell Seaton wanted them and the "Restless"? Now, as Dawson's active fingers pushed the pencil through the mazes of recorded messages, that active-minded young man began to get a glimpse.

"Sounds like something big, Joe," smiled Captain Tom, his eyes twinkling under the visor of his uniform cap as he thrust his head in through the doorway.

"It is," muttered Joe, in a low but tense voice. "Just wait. I've got one to send."

His fingers moved busily at the key for a little while. Then, snatching up the sheets of paper on which he had written, Joe Dawson leaped to his feet in such haste that he sent the chair spinning across the room.

Such impulsiveness in Dawson was so utterly unusual that Captain Tom Halstead gasped.

"Come on!" called Joe, darting to the door. "Down to the boat!"

"Where—?" began Tom Halstead, but he got only as far as that word, for Joe shot back:

"To sea!"

"How—" again essayed Halstead.

"At full speed—the fastest we can travel!" called back Joe, who was leaping down the porch steps.

"Any time to lock up?" demanded Tom, half-laughingly.

"Yes—but hustle! I'll get the motor started and be waiting."

Hank Butts was leaning indolently against one of the porch posts.

"Look at old Joe sailing before a fair wind," he laughed, admiringly.

"Turn to, Hank! Help lock the windows and the doors—full speed ahead!" directed Captain Tom, with vigor. "Joe Dawson never goes off at racing speed like that unless he has his orders and knows what he's doing."

"I thought you were the captain," grinned Hank, as he sprang to obey.

"So I am," Halstead shot at the other boy. "But, just as it happens, Joe has the sailing orders—and he can be trusted with 'em. Now—everything is tight and the keys in my pocket. For the dock, on the run!"

Chug-chug! Joe had surely been moving, for, by the time the other boys reached the dock, Dawson had the hatchway of the motor room open and the twin motors had begun to move. The young engineer, an oil-can in hand, was watching the revolutions of the two handsome machines.

"Stand by the stern-line to throw off, Hank," called Captain Tom, as he raced out onto the dock and made a plunge for the bow hawser. With this in hand he sprang aboard.

"How soon, Joe?" called the young skipper, throwing the canvas cover from the wheel down onto the bridge deck.

"As soon as you like," was Joe's answer, as he threw more speed into the twin motors.

Hank had the stern hawser in his hands by this time. Halstead threw the wheel over slightly, warping the boat's graceful bow away from the dock under just a touch of speed ahead.

"Come aboard, Hank!" called the young skipper. As soon as Butts had obeyed with a flying leap, Tom rang for half speed ahead, moving smoothly out of the little sand-bound harbor.

"Coil the hawsers, Hank," directed the young skipper. "Put the wheel cover away. Then relieve Joe. I want to hear from him."

These three separate orders Hank had executed within less than two minutes, and jumped down into the motor room. Joe came on deck, holding the sheets of paper in his hand.

"Now, let's understand what the business is, anyway," suggested Tom Halstead. "Who signaled us? Mr. Seaton?"

"Yes, but he wasn't the first one," Dawson answered. "The first hail came from out of the sea, from the Black B liner, 'Constant,' addressed to any wireless station and tagged 'urgent.' Here it is."

One hand on the wheel, the young skipper received the sheet held out to him. It read:

> Can you send fast boat instantly to take off badly injured
> passenger for medical treatment? Passenger A. B. Clodis, believed
> to be wealthy man from New York, discovered unconscious,
> perhaps dying, from fall. Fractured skull. Believe passenger or
> family to be able to pay handsomely for services.
>
> (Signed) HAMPTON, captain.

"Here's another sheet giving the ship's position at that moment," Joe continued; "also her course and speed."

"And you answered?" demanded Halstead.

"Just as I started to, the wireless at Beaufort broke in. It seems that Mr. Seaton is at Beaufort, and that he heard, at once, of the trouble. Here is Mr. Seaton's order."

Joe Dawson held out another sheet, on which he had transcribed this wireless message:

> Halstead, Lonely Island: Clodis is my man on important matter.
> Get him off ship, and with all speed. Take him to Lonely Island,
> where I will arrive with surgeons and nurses. Get all his baggage
> and papers off with him, and take greatest care of same. Whole thing
> plotted by enemies. If they succeed it spells ruin for me and more
> than one tragedy. I depend on you boys; don't fail me! Act at full
> speed.
>
> (Signed) POWELL SEATON.

P. XXX S.

"That comes from Mr. Seaton, all right," nodded Captain Tom. "That's his private signal, below his name, that he told us to look for on all orders of his. Now, let me have a look again at the position and course of the 'Constant.'"

After studying the dispatch intently, Captain Halstead nodded to his chum to take the wheel. Facing about, Tom swung open the small chart-case secured to the top of the deck-house. With a small, accurate pocket rule he made some measurements.

"At twenty-five miles an hour, Joe, if you can keep it up, a straight sou'east by east course should bring us right in the path of the 'Constant' on the course and speed she reports."

"Oh, we can keep the speed up," predicted Joe, confidently. "But I can't fool with the engine, unless you insist. I ought to be back in the cabin, at the wireless instrument."

"Hank can keep at the motors, then," nodded Captain Tom. "Go along, old fellow."

Joe paused but an instant to give Hank the needed orders, then raced aft. At the after end of the cabin were two snug little staterooms; at the other end, forward, a table had been fitted up with wireless apparatus, for the twin motors of the boat generated, by means of a dynamo, electricity enough for a very respectable wireless spark.

Hardly had Joe vanished when Hank, satisfied with the performance of the motors, appeared on deck. The signal mast stood just behind the bridge deck. It was of light, hollow steel, with two inner tubes that, when extended, made an unusually high mast for such a boat.

"We can run the extension mast up to full height in this light breeze, can't we, Tom?" asked the Long Island boy. Halstead nodded.

So simple was the arrangement that, within a few moments, Hank had the aerials well aloft. Nor was he too soon, for this query came promptly through space from Powell Seaton, up at Beaufort:

"Are you starting at once?"

With a quiet grin, all alone there by the wireless apparatus, young Dawson sparked back through the air:

"Three miles east, and running to intercept the 'Constant.'"

"Good!" came clicking into Joe Dawson's watch-case receivers against his ears, a moment later. "Then I won't bother you further. I trust you. But, oh, if you should fail! You don't know what failure means—to me!"

All this, of course, was clicked out in the dot and dash code of the Morse alphabet, but to Joe Dawson it was as plain as words spoken by the human voice.

"You're right, Mr. Seaton." Joe's busy right hand fingers clicked out the message on the sending key, while the electric waves sped from the aerials aloft outside. "We don't know what 'failure' means. We won't fail you. Good-bye."

Then Joe turned his attention to the "Constant." The big Black B liner answered promptly. She was on the same course, and glad to know that the "Restless" was speeding over the sea to seek her.

Having finished in raising the extended signal mast, and glancing into the motor room to see that the motors were running smoothly, Hank leaned against the raised deck top. The Long Island boy was hardly to be expected as a member of the crew of the "Restless" on this cruise, but he had wound up the summer season at East Hampton, and now, with idle September coming upon him, he had found the longing for the broad sea too powerful for him. Family conditions at home being satisfactory, he had promised himself this one month away from home, and was aboard as steward and general helper.

"I wonder if our work for Mr. Seaton has started in earnest?" ventured Hank.

"It has, for a few hours to-day, anyway," smiled Captain Tom. "We're cruising at full speed, and under orders from the man who chartered the 'Restless' for this month."

"But who can this Clodis be?"

"I don't know," Tom Halstead admitted.

"I wonder why Mr. Seaton is so mightily interested in him? What does Seaton mean by hinting at ruin and tragedies?"

"Do you know what I think, Hank?" queried the young skipper, quietly.

"What?"

"I think it would be downright impudence on our part to get too inquisitive about the affairs of the man who employs us. We looked Mr. Seaton up, and found he had the reputation of being an honest man. That's as much of his business as we have any right to want to know."

Hank colored, though he went on, in an argumentative way:

"I s'pose that's all true enough, Tom. Still, it's human nature, when you smell a big mystery, to want to know the meaning of at least some of it. And I'm mighty curious, because I scent something unusually big in the air."

"So do I," admitted the young skipper, giving the wheel another turn in order to hold the fast-moving boat to her course.

"Then what—"

"Hold on, Hank! Don't be downright nosey. And, as for guessing—"

"Why, Seaton as good as hints that there's been a downright attempt to kill this man Clodis," broke in Hank, who could not be repressed easily. "And Seaton is surely mightily worked up about it. And sending us out to take a passenger off a steamer bound for South America! Tom, do you s'pose that criminals are—"

"Hank," broke in the young skipper, half-severely, "there's something squeaking on one of the motors. For goodness' sake don't let us break down on what we've been told is a life-and-death trip! Get below and see what's wrong. Stand by to watch the performance of the motors."

Hank vanished, inwardly grumbling, for his curiosity was doing two hours' work every minute.

Captain Tom, after measuring on the chart, had figured on meeting the "Constant" in two hours and twenty minutes. Now, at every turn of the twin shafts the young skipper's blood bounded with the desire to do his full duty in arriving on time. Yet there was not wanting pleasure, mixed with the anxiety. How good the fresh, salty air tasted, out here on the broad sea, with the low coast-line already nearly out of sight! Tom Halstead sniffed in breath after breath. His eyes danced as they beheld the spraying of white water cut and turned up by the boat's fast prow. Oh, it was great to be out here on the deep, one hand guiding the course of one of the nimblest yachts afloat!

Joe, as he came forward, felt this same wild exhilaration. Quiet, dutiful and law-abiding as both these Motor Boat Club boys were, there must have been much of the old Norseman Viking blood in their veins, for this swift dash over the rolling swell of the ocean was like a tonic to them both.

"Say, isn't it all grand?" demanded Joe, his cheeks glowing, as he paused on the bridge deck, taking in great whiffs of the purest air supplied to man.

"Great!" admitted Skipper Tom, in a tone that was almost a cheer. Then he asked, gravely:

"Any news?"

"Mr. Seaton knows we have started, and expresses his pleasure. I've signaled the 'Constant,' and she's still keeping to the same course, and will so continue."

"And the patient, Clodis?"

"Still alive, Tom; but the ship's surgeon offers no hope, and will be glad to have us take him onto the 'Restless.'"

"It must be something terrible to make Mr. Seaton so anxious about the man," observed Tom, thoughtfully.

"Yes," nodded Joe. Then: "Say, Tom, I've just struck an easy scheme for connecting one of the armatures of the Morse register, aft, to a buzzer in the engine room. Then if I happen to be in the engine room when wireless messages are traveling through the air I shall know it."

In the next hour all three of the boys, though they did not talk much about it, were wondering about this tragedy of the deep sea that had called them into action. Though they could not as yet guess it, this present affair of theirs was but the start of a series of adventures more amazing than any they had ever dreamed of. Now, at the most, they were curious. Soon they were to know what it meant to be astounded; they were soon to know what it felt like to feel haunted, to find themselves assailed by dread after dread. Undoubtedly it was merciful for them that they could not, at this moment, peer behind the curtain of the immediate future.

So, ignorant of what fate and destiny held in store for them, they were mainly intent, now, upon intercepting at the right point the big liner cruising swiftly southward.

In another hour they made out smoke on the horizon where Skipper Tom judged the "Constant" to be. Later the spars of the steamship were visible through the marine glasses. Then the hull appeared. A few minutes later Captain Tom ran the "Restless" dashingly in alongside the great black hull of the liner, along whose starboard rail a hundred or more passengers had gathered.

Turning the wheel over to Hank, Captain Tom Halstead snatched up the megaphone as the larger vessel slowed down.

"'Constant,' ahoy!" bellowed the young skipper. "This is the yacht 'Restless,' sent to receive your injured passenger, Clodis."

"'Restless' ahoy!" came the response from the liner's bridge. "We'll lower our starboard side gangway, if you can come alongside safely."

The Motor Boat Club boys were at the threshold of their strangest, wildest succession of adventures!

CHAPTER II
SOME OF THE MYSTERY UNRAVELED

"IF we can come alongside safely," echoed Hank, disgustedly. "I'll show 'em—and in a smooth swell of sea like this, too!"

As the big steamship lay to, Hank steered in until Captain Tom, boathook in hand, made fast temporarily. Then Hank hurried up with a line with which he took a fast hitch.

"Hey, there, you'll pull away our side gangway," roared down a mate, whose head and uniform cap showed over the rail above.

"You don't know us," grinned Joe Dawson, quietly.

By this time Tom Halstead was running lightly up the steps of the gangway. He reached the small platform above, then passed to the deck.

He was met by Captain Hampton, who inquired:

"Where's your sailing master, young man?"

"Right before you, Captain."

"You?"

"Yes, sir."

"Who are your owners?" demanded Captain Hampton, much astonished by Tom's quiet assurance.

"I'm captain and half-owner of the 'Restless,' sir," Halstead continued, still smiling at the other captain's very evident astonishment. "The other owner is the engineer, Joe Dawson, my chum."

Captain Hampton swallowed something very hard. Several of the passengers were smiling. A man who has followed the sea for years knows the capacity and efficiency that boys often display on shipboard, but it is unusual to find a boy acting as master of a yacht.

However, there was the "Restless," and there was Tom Halstead in the captain's uniform. These were facts that could not be disputed.

"You have a passenger, a Mr. Clodis, that you want to have me take off?" resumed Tom.

"Yes; you have come for him, then?"

"Not only that, but Mr. Seaton, the gentleman who has our boat in charter, has very urgently ordered us to bring Mr. Clodis ashore; also his baggage complete, and any and all papers that he may have brought aboard."

"You have a comfortable berth on your boat?"

"Several of them," Tom answered.

"Then I'll have some of my men make the transfer at once. Our ship's surgeon, Dr. Burke, will also go over the side and see that Mr. Clodis is made as comfortable as possible for his trip ashore."

"Steward Butts will show your men to the port stateroom, aft, sir."

11

A mate hurried away to give the order to Dr. Burke. A boatswain was directed to attend to having all of Mr. Clodis's baggage go over the side.

"Come to my stateroom, sir, if you please," requested Captain Hampton, and Tom followed.

"When you take a man with a fractured skull ashore, the authorities may want some explanation," declared the 'Constant's' sailing master, opening his desk. "Here is a statement, therefore, that I have prepared and signed. Take it with you, Captain—"

"Halstead," supplied Tom.

The motor boat boy glanced hurriedly through the document.

"I see you state it was an accident, Captain Hampton," went on Halstead, lowering his voice. "Our charter-man, Mr. Seaton, intimated that he believed it might have been a deliberate assault. Have you anything that you wish to say on this point, sir?"

"I don't believe it was an assault," replied the ship's master, musingly. Halstead's quick eye noted that Hampton appeared to be a sturdy, honest sea-dog. "Still, Captain Halstead, if you would like to question the steward who found Mr. Clodis at the foot of the main saloon companionway—"

"Have you made the investigation thoroughly, sir?"

"I think so—yes."

"Then nothing is likely to be gained, Captain, by my asking any questions of a steward you have already questioned."

The mate came back to report that Mr. Clodis had been carried over the side, and that his baggage had been taken aboard the "Restless."

"I know you don't want a liner held up," Tom went on, slipping Captain Hampton's report of the accident into his pocket. "I'll go over the side, sir, as soon as you can ascertain whether Mr. Clodis had any papers that ought to be sent ashore with him."

"There are none in the injured man's pockets," replied the steamship's sailing master, "and none were deposited with the purser. So, if there are any papers, they must be in Mr. Clodis's trunk or bag."

"Thank you, sir. Then I'll bid you good-bye and hurry over the side," said Halstead, energetically.

As they stepped out of the stateroom a passenger who had been lingering near stepped up.

"Oh, one moment," said Captain Hampton, suddenly. "Captain Halstead, this gentleman is Mr. Arthur Hilton. Since leaving New York he has received some wireless news that makes him anxious to return. He wants to go ashore with you."

Arthur Hilton had stepped forward, holding out his hand, which Tom took in his own. Mr. Hilton was a man of about thirty, smooth-faced, with firm set jaws. Though evidently not a Spaniard, he had the complexion usual to that race. His dark eyes were keen and sharp, though they had a rather pleasant look in them. He was slender, perhaps five feet eight inches tall, and, although his waist and legs were thin, he had broad, rather powerful looking shoulders.

"You can set me ashore, can't you, young man, for a ten-dollar bill?" inquired Hilton.

"Certainly, if Captain Hampton knows no reason why you shouldn't leave the vessel," Tom answered.

"Mr. Hilton has surrendered his passage ticket, and there is nothing to detain him aboard," replied the steamship's master.

"Your baggage ready, sir?" asked Tom.

"Nothing but this bag," laughed Hilton, stepping back and picking up his hand luggage.

"Come along, then, sir."

As Tom Halstead pressed his way through the throng of passengers gathered on deck, he heard several wondering, and some admiring, remarks relative to the youthfulness of the skipper of so handsome and trim a yacht.

Hilton followed the young skipper down over the side. Tom turned to help him to the deck of the "Restless," but Hilton lightly leaped across, holding his bag before him. Tom Halstead, as he turned, got a good look at that bag. It was one that he was likely to remember for many a day. The article was of dark red leather, and on one side the surface for a space as large as a man's hand had been torn away, probably in some accident.

"Here's the passage money, Captain," said Hilton, passing over a ten-dollar bill. Murmuring his thanks, the young skipper crumpled up the bill, shoving it into a trousers pocket, then hurried aft.

Clodis was a short, almost undersized man of perhaps forty-five, stout and well dressed. His head was so bandaged, as he lay in the lower berth of the port stateroom, that not much of his face was visible.

"He's unconscious, and probably will be for hours," stated Dr. Burke, as Captain Tom appeared in the doorway. "If he comes to, I've left some medicine with your steward, to be given the patient. Of course you'll get him ashore and under medical care as promptly as possible, Captain."

"Surgeons are on the way from Beaufort to meet us," the young skipper nodded.

"Then I'll return to my ship," declared Dr. Burke, rising. "But I'm glad to know that Mr. Clodis is going to be met by a friend."

As the doctor hurried over the side, Hilton turned to walk aft.

"Stay forward, if you please, sir," interposed Captain Tom. "No one is to go into the cabin until the patient has been removed under a doctor's orders."

There was a frown on Hilton's face, which, however, almost instantly vanished. Joe brought a deck arm chair and placed it for Mr. Hilton on the bridge deck.

"Good luck for you and your patient, sir," called down Captain Hampton over the rail, as he prepared to get under headway.

"Thank you, sir," Tom acknowledged. "We'll take the best care of Mr. Clodis that we know how."

With Hank on duty in the cabin, Tom Halstead had to cast off and make his own start as best he could. He managed the double task neatly, however, and, as he fell away the "Constant's" engine-room bell could be heard for half-speed-ahead.

The little auto-whistle of the "Restless" sounded shrilly, to be answered with a long, deep-throated blast from the liner's steam whistle. With this brief interchange of sea courtesies the two craft fell apart, going on their respective ways.

"Full speed on the return?" called Joe, from the doorway of the motor room.

"Yes," nodded Captain Tom. "But look out for vibration. Our sick man has had his skull cracked."

By the time the yacht had gone scooting for more than a mile over the waves, Captain Halstead, left hand on the wheel, turned to Hilton.

"Did you hear how our sick man came to be hurt, sir?"

"I didn't hear of it until a couple of hours after it happened," replied Hilton. "I understand that Mr. Clodis fell down the stairs leading to the main saloon, and was picked up unconscious. That was about all the word that was given out on board."

Captain Tom nodded, then gave his whole attention to making Lonely Island as speedily as possible. There was no land in sight, and the trip back was a long one. Yet the young skipper had his bearings perfectly.

They were still some eight miles off Lonely Island when Hilton roused himself at sight of a low-hulled, black schooner scudding north under a big spread of canvas.

"You're going to pass close to that boat, aren't you, Captain?" asked the bridge deck passenger.

"Yes, sir; pretty close."

"As I understand it, you're going to land at an island some miles off the coast, whereas I wish to reach the mainland at the earliest possible moment, and catch a railway train. So, Captain, if you'll signal that schooner and put me aboard, I shall feel under sufficient obligation to hand you another ten-dollar bill."

That looked so much like earning money rapidly that Halstead called Joe up from the motor room to set the signal. The schooner lay to until overtaken. Hilton discovered that the schooner was bound for Beaufort, and the bargain was quickly completed. A small boat put off from the sailing vessel and the bridge deck passenger, his noticeable bag included, was transferred.

The "Restless" was nearer Lonely Island, and the schooner was hull down, when Captain Tom suddenly started as Joe Dawson stepped upon deck.

"Blazes, Joe!" exclaimed the young skipper. "I'm afraid we've done it!"

"I'm afraid so, too," came quietly from the young engineer.

"That fellow Hilton, so anxious to get ashore, may be the very chap who struck down Mr. Clodis!"

"The thought had just come to me," admitted Joe.

"Yes! You know, Mr. Seaton hinted that the 'accident' might have been an attempt to kill."

Captain and engineer of the "Restless" stared disconcertedly at each other.

"Now, why did I have to go and make such a fearful stumble as that?" groaned Tom.

"You didn't, any more than I did," Joe tried to console him.

"We should, at least, have kept Hilton aboard until Mr. Seaton had had a chance to look him over."

"I could send a wireless to the Beaufort police to grab Hilton on landing," suggested Joe, doubtfully, but Tom Halstead shook his head energetically.

"No; the Beaufort police wouldn't do that on our say-so, Joe. And, even if they did, we might get ourselves into a lot of trouble."

The "Restless" kept smoothly, swiftly on her way, bounding over the low, gentle swell of the calm ocean. Tom shivered whenever he thought of the possibility of the motors becoming cranky. With such important human freight aboard any mishap to the machinery would be extremely serious.

"Joe," called Tom, at last, as the yacht came in sight of Lonely Island, "there's a tug at our dock."

Dawson came on deck, taking the marine glass from his chum's hand.

"I guess Mr. Seaton has been hustling, then. He couldn't have come from Beaufort on the tug, after all the trouble of rounding up doctors. He must have come down the shore in an automobile, and then engaged the tug near the island."

As the "Restless" went closer, the tug, with two short toots of its whistle, moved out from the dock. Powell Seaton, in broad-brimmed hat and blue serge, waved his hand vigorously at the boys. With him stood three men, presumably surgeons. Captain Tom Halstead sounded three short blasts of the auto-whistle to signal the success of his errand, while Joe swung his uniform cap over his head.

"Get down to your engines, Joe," called Captain Tom. "I'm going to make a swift landing that will be in keeping with Mr. Seaton's impatience."

Up to within nearly two hundred yards of the dock the "Restless" dashed in at full speed. Then signaling for half speed, next for the stop, and finally for the reverse, Captain Tom swung the yacht in almost a semi-circle, running up with bare headway so that the boat lay in gently against the string-piece. In that instant Tom, leaving the wheel, bounded up onto the dock, bow hawser in hand, and made the loop fast over the snubbing post. In the same instant Joe Dawson, cat-footed, raced aft, next leaping ashore with the stern hawser.

"Jove, but that was a beautiful bit of boat-handling—a superb piece of seamanship!" muttered one of the surgeons, admiringly.

Powell Seaton, however, stopped to hear none of this. He gripped Tom by the arm, demanding hoarsely:

"You brought Clodis ashore? How is he? Where?"

"Still unconscious, sir, and the ship's doctor offered no hope. You will find your friend in the port stateroom, sir."

Signing to the surgeons to accompany him, Mr. Seaton vanished aft, the medical men with him. Ten minutes passed before Hank came up, alone.

"What do the doctors say, Hank?" demanded Tom, instantly.

"One chance in about a million," replied Hank, in a very subdued voice—for him.

Five minutes later Mr. Seaton, hat in hand, also came up on deck.

"Mr. Seaton," murmured Tom, eagerly, "I've been waiting for you. I—we've something to tell you." Then the young skipper detailed the affair of taking Arthur Hilton from the "Constant" and transferring him to the Beaufort-bound schooner.

"Describe the fellow!" commanded Powell Seaton, suddenly, hoarsely.

Captain Tom did so.

"Arthur Hilton he called himself, did he?" cried Mr. Seaton, in a rage. "Anson Dalton is the scoundrel's real name!"

"Who is he, sir?" Tom asked, anxiously.

"Who is Anson Dalton?" cried Mr. Seaton, his voice sounding as though he were choking. "Who, but the scoundrel who has engineered this whole desperate plot against me! The dastard who struck down Allan Clodis! The knave who has striven for the badge of Cain!"

CHAPTER III
INVISIBLE HANDS AT THE WIRELESS

In a rear bedroom, the furthest apartment from the wireless room of the bungalow, Allan Clodis, barely alive, was placed when they bore him up from the boat. Then the three surgeons, retaining only Hank Butts, drove the others from the room.

"Back to the wireless!" breathed Seaton, tensely. "Dawson, get Beaufort on the jump."

"I have the Beaufort operator," reported Joe, after a few moments.

"Then rush this message, and ask the operator to get it in the hands of the chief of police without an instant's loss of time," directed Mr. Seaton, speaking in jerky haste.

The message described Anson Dalton, also the black schooner on which he had last been seen. The police chief was asked to arrest Dalton on sight, on the authority of Powell Seaton, and hold him for the United States authorities, for an attempt at homicide on an American ship on the high seas.

Within ten minutes back came the reply from Beaufort to this effect:

"I have men out watching for the schooner. Man Dalton will be arrested as you request. Will notify you."

"Good!" cried Mr. Seaton, rubbing his hands vengefully. "Oh, Dalton, you scoundrel, you can't escape us now, for long! You knew that, if you continued down the coast, there was danger that a United States revenue cutter would intercept the ship and take you off. At best, you knew you would be arrested at Rio Janeiro, if I suspected you, as I was bound to do. So you tried to steal ashore here, to be swallowed up in the mazes of this broad country at least an hour or two ahead of pursuit. And, but for the wireless spark that leaps through space, you could have done so. But we shall have you now."

"Unless—" began Tom Halstead, hintingly, then paused.

"Unless—what?" insisted Mr. Seaton.

"Suppose Dalton is shrewd enough to pay the captain of the schooner to land him at some other point, where there is neither a policeman nor a telegraph station?"

Seaton made a noise that sounded as though he were grinding his teeth. Then he picked up a pencil, writing furiously.

"Send this to the police chief at Beaufort," he ordered. Joe Dawson's fingers made the sending-key sing. The message was one warning the police chief that Dalton might attempt to land at some point outside of Beaufort, and asking him to cover all near points along the coast. Mr. Seaton offered to make good any expense that this would entail.

Once more, in a few minutes, the answer was at hand.

"Chief of police at Beaufort says," Joe translated the dots and dashes, "that his authority does not extend beyond the city limits."

Again Mr. Seaton began to show signs of fury. Then, as though to force self-control, he trod softly out of the room, going toward the door of the sick-room, where Hank Butts stood guard.

"No news, sir; no change," Hank reported, in an undertone.

"I'm afraid Mr. Seaton is pretty angry with us," said Tom Halstead, gravely, "for allowing Hilton—Dalton, I mean—to get away from us."

"Then he may as well get over it," commented Joe Dawson, quietly. "We're hired to furnish a boat, to sail it, and, incidentally, to run a wireless telegraph apparatus. We didn't engage ourselves as policemen."

"True," nodded young Captain Halstead. "Still, I might have done some quicker thinking. My! What would Dalton have felt like if I had run straight for this dock, refusing to put him aboard any other craft?"

"If you had tried to do that," retorted Joe, with another quiet smile, "do you know, Tom, what I think your friends would have been doing and saying of you?"

"No; of course not."

"Your friends would have been sending flowers, and bringing tears. They would be looking at you, to-morrow, and saying, in undertones: 'Goodness, how natural he looks!'"

Halstead was puzzled for a moment or two. Then, comprehending, he grinned, though he demanded:

"You think Dalton would have dared anything like that?"

"Well, you notice what kind of a rascal Mr. Seaton thinks Dalton is. And you know we don't go armed aboard the 'Restless.' Now, I'm pretty certain that Dalton could have displayed and used weapons if we had given him any cause to do so."

Ten minutes later, when Powell Seaton entered the room, he beheld Captain Tom Halstead seated at the operator's table, sealing an envelope that he had just directed.

"What are you doing, Captain?" asked the charter-man.

"You know that miserable twenty dollars that I took from Anson Dalton for passage money?" inquired Halstead, looking up.

"Yes."

"I've just enclosed the money in this envelope, with a note."

"Going to return the money to Dalton when you find his address?" smiled Mr. Seaton, wearily.

"No, sir," retorted Tom, in a voice sharp with disgust. "Dalton seems to have more money, already, than is good for him. I've addressed this envelope to a county institution down in the state that I come from."

"A public institution?"

"Yes, sir; the home for feeble-minded youth."

"Don't take it so hard as that, Halstead," urged Mr. Seaton. "Had you had a suspicion you would have done whatever lay in your power. I might have warned you against Dalton, but the truth is, *I* did not imagine he would be right on the scene."

Saying which, Powell Seaton walked away by himself. He was gravely, even sadly preoccupied. Though Captain Halstead could not even guess what the underlying mystery was, he knew that it seriously affected Mr. Seaton's plans and fortune. Their charter-man was worried almost past endurance, though bravely trying to hide the fact.

After the consultation of the surgeons, two of them departed aboard the tug, the third remaining to care for the patient. Hank, despite all his bluntness of manner, was proving himself valuable in the sick-room, while Joe spent most of his time in the wireless room of the bungalow, waiting to receive or send any word. So, as evening came, Tom Halstead bestirred himself with the preparation of the evening meal.

By dark there was a considerable wind blowing. Halstead left his cooking long enough to run down and make sure that all was snug and tight aboard the "Restless." The young skipper had fairly to fight his way against the wind on his return to the bungalow.

"There's going to be a tough old gale to-night," Tom muttered to himself, as he halted, a moment, on the porch, to study the weather conditions.

As yet, it was blowing only fairly hard. As the little group at the bungalow seated themselves at supper, however, the storm broke, with a deluge of rain and a sharp roar of thunder.

"This will bother wireless conditions to-night, won't it?" queried Mr. Seaton, as they ate.

"Some, perhaps, if the gale and the storm keep up," replied Joe Dawson. "But I imagine the worst of the gale is passing now."

And so it proved. An hour later the rain was falling steadily, though only in a drizzle. The wind had moderated a good deal.

As all hands, save Hank, sat in the sitting room of the bungalow, after the meal, the warning bell from the apparatus room suddenly tinkled.

"You see, sir," said Joe, rising quickly, "the wireless is still able to work."

He passed into the next room, seating himself by the instruments and slipping on the head-band that held the receivers.

"From Beaufort, sir," Joe said, presently, looking up. "The police report that no such schooner has landed at that city."

"Acknowledge the message of the police," directed Mr. Seaton, "and ask them not to give up the lookout through the night. Tell the chief of police that I'll gladly meet any expense that may be incurred."

Joe's right hand reached out for the sending-key. Then a blank look flashed across his face.

"Something wrong with the sending-key connections," he explained, in a low voice, leaping up. He examined the connections closely, yet, the more he looked, the more puzzled he became.

"The storage batteries can't have given out," he muttered, snatching up a lighted lantern. "But I'll go and look at them."

Out into the little dynamo shed he darted, followed by Powell Seaton and by Tom. The doctor was dozing in an arm-chair.

Joe gave two or three swift looks at the dynamo, the storage battery connections and other parts of the apparatus. Then his face went white with rage.

"Look here, Mr. Seaton," he panted, hoarsely. "There's been some infernal work here—someone else has been on the island, for none of our crowd would do such a trick! Not even in fun! Look, sir, at where the parts have been tampered with. Look where pliers have been used to cut the wire connections. See where these two bolts have been neatly removed with the help of wrenches. Look at—"

Joe paused, then glanced wildly around.

"Great Scott!" he groaned. "Just the parts removed that can't be replaced. The whole generating plant crippled! Mr. Seaton, until we get in touch with the mainland, and get some needed supplies there, we can't use this wireless plant again. We can receive messages—yes, up to any limit, but not a word can we send away from here."

"But who can have done this trick?" gasped Powell Seaton, looking as though amazement had numbed him, as, indeed, it almost had.

"Someone has landed here, since dark," broke in Tom Halstead, all a-quiver with dismay. "While we were at supper some sneak or sneaks have landed on this island. They have pried their way in here, and they've crippled our connection with the outside world."

"They could do it all easily enough, without making any noise," confirmed Joe. "Yes—they've done a splendid job, from a scoundrel's point of view!"

"Then you can't make this apparatus work for the sending of even a single message?" demanded Mr. Seaton.

"Not until we've landed some necessary repair and replacement materials from the mainland," replied Joe, with a disgusted shake of his head.

"But you can still send messages from the 'Restless,'" hinted Powell Seaton.

Tom Halstead bounded for the door of the dynamo shed with a sudden exclamation of dread.

"We can use the boat's wireless," nodded Joe, following, and speaking over his shoulder, "unless the same crowd of rascals have broken into the boat's motor room or cabin and played us the same trick there."

In the big sitting room, beside the large open fire-place, was a pile of long sticks of firewood. Tom Halstead stopped to snatch up one of these, and Joe quickly followed suit.

19

"I'll go down to the boat with you, boys," said Mr. Seaton, who had followed them. "If there's anyone around to put up a fight you'll want some help."

But Captain Tom, acting, for the moment, as though he were aboard the yacht, suddenly took command.

"Mr. Seaton," he said, "you'd better remain here to guard your unconscious friend. Doctor, wake up! Better go in and send Hank Butts out on the trot. We'll take him with us."

Dr. Cosgrove, awaking and realizing that something important was happening, swiftly moved off to the sick-room. Hank was speedily out with his comrades.

"If there are rascals on this island, who have designs against you, Mr. Seaton, then mount guard over your friend," Tom added. "Better be in the sick-room at any moment when Dr. Cosgrove leaves there. Hank, get a club from that pile. Now, come along, fellows, and we'll see what infernal mischief may have been done to the 'Restless.'"

With that, the young skipper bounded out onto the porch, thence running down the board walk toward the dock.

Tom Halstead had some vague but highly uneasy notions as to the safety of his beloved boat. Yet, alarmed as he was, he was hardly prepared for the shock that met him when he arrived at the edge of the little wharf.

"Say, can you beat that?" panted young Halstead, halting, thunderstruck, and gazing back at his stupefied comrades. "The rascals—whoever they are—have stolen the 'Restless.' Joe, our splendid boat is gone!"

CHAPTER IV
TAKING A GREAT CHANCE

Joe, with a voiceless gulp, sprang forward once more, pausing at the string-piece only, and peering hard out into the black, wet night.

Hank Butts brought his club down over a snubbing post with such force as to shatter the weapon.

For a few moments Tom Halstead stood looking about him in an uncertain way, as though trying to arouse himself from a hideous nightmare.

"They've stolen our boat!" he gasped.

Whoever had done this deed might almost as well have taken the young captain's life. The "Restless" was a big part of that life.

"Oh, well," muttered Hank, thickly, "whoever took the yacht must leave it somewhere. You can't hide a craft of that size. We'll hear from the 'Restless' all right, in a day or two—or in a week, anyway."

"Whoever took the yacht away from here may know next to nothing about handling a boat," choked Tom, hoarsely. "We may find the dear old craft again—yes—but perhaps wedged on the rocks somewhere,—a hopeless wreck. O-o-oh! It makes me feel ugly and heartsick, all in one!"

"The 'Restless' can't have broken loose during the storm, can it?" asked Hank Butts.

"No," retorted Tom and Joe in the same breath, and with the utmost positiveness.

20

"Well, what are we going to do?" asked Hank.

The answer to the question was hard to find. Lonely Island lay five miles off the shore. Wireless communication was out of the question. They were out of the track of passing vessels, nor was any stray, friendly craft at all likely to show up on this dark, forbidding night.

"Come on back, fellows," said Tom, chokingly. "There's nothing we can do here, and Mr. Seaton must know the whole situation."

The owner of the bungalow listened to them with a blank face when the Motor Boat Club boys again stood before him.

"I can't even guess what to make out of this," he confessed.

"It would help Dalton greatly if Mr. Clodis died to-night, wouldn't it, sir?" inquired the young skipper.

"It would help Dalton much, and be of still greater value to the wretches behind Dalton," replied Mr. Seaton, grinding his teeth.

"Then, sir, as the tug went back to mainland with two of the doctors, isn't it possible that some spy may have concluded that *all* the doctors had returned until summoned again?"

"That seems very likely," nodded the owner of the bungalow.

"Then perhaps Dalton—and those behind him—hope that Mr. Clodis will become much worse, and die before you can again summon help from the mainland."

"That looks more likely than any other explanation of these strange happenings," agreed Mr. Seaton, studying the floor, while the frown on his face deepened.

"And the scoundrels," quavered Tom, "may even come back during the night and try to make *sure* that Mr. Clodis dies without ever becoming conscious."

"I don't quite see why they need care so much," replied Mr. Seaton, slowly. "Dalton got all of Clodis's papers—the ones that I wanted preserved from the wretches back of Dalton."

"Are you sure they have *all?*" propounded Captain Halstead.

"Why, Clodis carried the papers in a money-belt, and, in undressing him, we found that belt gone."

"Have you looked through the baggage that we brought ashore with Mr. Clodis?"

"I haven't thought of it. Haven't had time," replied Mr. Seaton. "But I will now. Mr. Clodis's steamer trunk is in the room with him. We'll bring it out, and search."

Tom and Hank brought the trunk out.

"The lock hasn't been tampered with, you see, sir," suggested Halstead.

"Here are Clodis's keys," replied Powell Seaton, producing a ring. One of the keys he fitted to the trunk lock, next throwing up the lid. After rummaging for a few moments, Mr. Seaton brought up a sealed envelope from the bottom of the trunk.

"Dalton *would* have been glad to get this," he cried, with a near approach to delight.

"Lock it up tight in your innermost pockets then, sir," counseled Tom Halstead. "The contents of that envelope must be what Dalton has come back here for, or sent someone else for. And, until he gets it, he must plan to keep Lonely Island out of touch with the whole world. We'll hear from him again to-night, I'm thinking."

"Will we?" flared Mr. Seaton, stepping briskly across the room. Unlocking a cupboard door, he brought out a repeating shot-gun. From an ammunition box he helped himself to several shells, fitting six of them into the magazine of the gun.

"Buckshot talks, sometimes," said the owner of the bungalow, more quietly. "I shall be awake to-night, and have this gun always with me."

"Have you any other weapons, sir?" asked Tom.

"Yes; a revolver—here it is."

Powell Seaton held out the weapon, but Halstead shook his head.

"Dr. Cosgrove is the one who'll want that, since he must stay by Mr. Clodis to-night. And, see here, Mr. Seaton, impress upon the doctor that he mustn't take a nap, even for a moment. As for you, you'll want to be watching the house in general."

"Why, where will you young men be?" inquired Mr. Seaton.

"We couldn't stay indoors, with our boat gone, sir," Tom answered. "The first thing we must do is to explore all around the island. Even if we don't get a sign of the 'Restless,' we may find out something else. We may be able to catch someone trying to land on this island later to-night."

"Yes; it will be best to have guards outside roaming about the island," admitted Powell Seaton, readily. Then, lowering his voice as he signed to the Motor Boat Club boys to draw closer to him, Mr. Seaton added:

"Something, of some nature, *will* be attempted to-night. There is no other sound explanation of the crippling of the wireless and the stealing of the boat. So be vigilant, boys—as I shall also be while you're gone."

Hank helped himself to a fresh club—a stouter one than that which he had broken over the snubbing post at the dock. Then out into the black night fared the three Motor Boat Club boys.

"Shall we keep together, or spread?" asked Joe Dawson.

"Together," nodded Tom Halstead. "If there are prowlers about, we can't tell how soon three of us may be even too few. Remember, we have only firewood to fight with, and we don't know what kind of men we may run up against."

So Tom led his friends down to a point but little south of the dock. From here, following the shore, they started to prowl slowly around Lonely Island, all the while keeping a sharp watch to seaward.

"If the boat is in any waters near at hand we ought to get some sign of her whereabouts by keeping a sharp enough watch," Tom advised his comrades. "They can't sail or handle the boat without the occasional use of a light in the motor room. The gleam of a lantern across the water may be enough to give us an idea where she is."

Peering off into the blackness of the night, this seemed like rather a forlorn hope.

"If whoever has stolen the boat intends to land later to-night," hinted Joe, "it's much more likely that the thieves are, at this moment, a good, biggish distance away, so as not to give us any clew to their intentions."

In the course of twenty minutes the Motor Boat Club boys had made their way around to the southern end of the island.

Somewhat more than a mile to the southward lay a small, unnamed island. It was uninhabited, and too sandy to be of value to planters. Yet it had one good cove of rather deep water.

Tom halted, staring long and hard in the direction where he knew this little spot on the ocean to stand. It was too black a night for any glimpse of the island to be had against the sky.

"That would be a good enough place for our pirates to have taken the 'Restless,'" he muttered, to his comrades.

"If we only had a boat, we could know, bye-and-bye," muttered Hank, discontentedly.

"We have been known to swim further than that," said Joe, quietly.

"But never in such a sea as is running to-night," sighed Tom Halstead. "Even as the water is, I'd like to chance it, but I'm afraid it would be useless. And it would leave Mr. Seaton and the doctor alone against any surprise."

"I'd swim that far, or drown, even in this sea," muttered Dawson, vengefully, "if I had any idea that our boat lay over that way."

For two or three minutes the boys stood there, talking. Not once did Tom Halstead turn his eyes away from the direction of the island to the southward.

"Look there!" the young skipper finally uttered, clutching at Joe's elbow. "Did you see that?"

"Yes," voiced Joe, in instant excitement.

"That" was a tiny glow of light, made small by the distance.

"It's a lantern, being carried by someone," continued Captain Tom, after a breathless pause. "There—it vanishes! Oh, I say—gracious!"

Joe, too, gave a gasp.

As for Hank Butts, that youth commenced to breathe so hard that there was almost a rattle to his respiration.

Immediately following the disappearance of the distant light, four smaller, dimmer lights appeared, in a row.

"That's the same light, showing through the four starboard ports of the motor room," trembled Joe Dawson. "Starboard, because the lantern was carried forward, before it disappeared briefly in the hatchway of the motor room."

"That's our boat—there isn't a single doubt of it," cried Tom Halstead, enthusiastically. "And now—oh, fellows! We've simply got to swim over there, rough sea or smooth sea. We've got to get our own boat back unless the heavens fall on us on the way over!"

"Humph! What are we going to do," demanded Hank Butts, "if we find a gang aboard that we can't whip or bluff?"

"That," spoke Captain Tom, softly, "will have to be decided after we get there. But swim over there we must, since there isn't anything on this island that even looks like a boat. See here, Joe, you and Hank trot up to the bungalow and tell

Mr. Seaton what we've seen. The 'Restless' is at anchor in the cove yonder. There are plenty of logs up at the bungalow. Come back with one big enough to buoy us up in the water, yet not so big but what we can steer it while swimming. And bring with it a few lengths of that quarter-inch cord from the dynamo room. Don't be too long, will you, fellows?"

After Joe and Hank had departed, Tom Halstead watched the light shining behind the four distant ports until it disappeared. Then he looked at the waves long and wonderingly.

"It's a big chance to take. I don't know whether we can ever get out there in a sea like this," he muttered. "Yet, what wouldn't I do to get control of our own boat again? Our own boat—the good old 'Restless'! Joe isn't saying much of anything; he never does, but I know how he feels over the stealing of the boat and the chance that bunglers may leave her on the rocks somewhere along this coast!"

A few minutes passed. Then the young skipper heard hurrying footsteps. Joe and Hank hove into sight out of the deep gloom, bearing an eight-foot log on their shoulders.

"Good enough," nodded Halstead, eyeing the log approvingly. "Now, wade into the water with it, and let's see whether it will buoy us all up at need."

All three waded out with the log, until they were in nearly up to their shoulders.

"Now, hang to it, and see if it will hold us up," commanded Captain Tom Halstead.

The log bore them up, but the crest of a big wave, rolling in, hurled them back upon the beach. Tom dragged the log up onto dry ground.

"Now, first of all, let's lash our clubs to the log," suggested the young skipper. This was soon accomplished. Then each of the Motor Boat Club boys made a medium length of the cord fast around his chest, under the arm-pits.

"The next trick," proposed Halstead, "is to make the other end fast to the log, allowing just length enough so that you can swim well clear of the log itself, and yet be able to haul yourselves back to the log in case you find your strength giving out."

This took some calculation, but at last the three motor boat boys decided that eight feet of line was the proper length. This decided, and accomplished, they carried the log down into the water, and pushed resolutely off into the blackness.

Even Tom Halstead, who allowed himself few doubts, little believed that they could accomplish this long, dangerous swimming cruise over a rough sea.

CHAPTER V
TOM MATCHES ONE TRICK WITH ANOTHER

At the outset Joe swam at the rear, frequently giving a light push to send the log riding ahead. Tom and Hank swam on either side, half-towing the timber that was to be their buoy when needed.

All three, reared at the edge of salt water, as they had been, were strong, splendid swimmers. This night, however, with the rough waves, the feat was especially dangerous.

"Swim the way a fellow does when he knows he's really *got* to," was the young skipper's terse advice as they started.

It became a contest of endurance. Tom and Joe, the two Maine boys, were doggedly determined to reach their boat or perish in the attempt. Hank Butts, the Long Island boy, though perhaps possessing less fine courage than either of his comrades, had a rough way of treating danger as a joke. This may have been a pretense, yet in times of peril it passed well enough for grit.

Any one of the three could have swum a mile readily on a lightly rolling sea, but to-night the feat was a vastly sterner one. Hank was the first to give out, after going a little more than an eighth of the distance. He swam to the log, throwing his right arm over it and holding on while the two Maine boys pushed and towed it. Finally, when young Butts had broken away to swim, Joe closed in, holding to the log for a while. At last it came even doughty Tom Halstead's turn to seek this aid to buoyancy.

Nor had they covered half the distance, in all, when all three found themselves obliged to hold to the log, as it rolled and plunged, riding the waves. Worst of all, despite their exertions, all three now found their teeth chattering.

"Say, it begins to look like a crazy undertaking," declared Hank, with blunt candor. "Can we possibly make it?"

"We've got to," retorted Tom Halstead, his will power unshaken.

"I don't see the light over there any more," observed Hank, speaking the words in jerks of one syllable, so intense was the shaking of his jaws.

"Maybe the boat isn't over yonder any longer," admitted Captain Tom, "but we've got to chance it. And say, we'd better shove off and try to swim again, to warm ourselves up. We're in danger of shaking ourselves plum to pieces."

There was another great peril, on which none of them had calculated well enough before starting. When they were clear of the log, swimming, it pitched so on the tops of the waves that it was likely, at any instant, to drive against the head of one of the swimmers and crack his skull.

"If we had known all this before we started—" began Hank, the next time the three swimmers were driven to cling, briefly, to their movable buoy.

"We'd have started just the same," retorted Tom, as stiffly as his chattering teeth would let him speak.

"Humph!" muttered Hank, unbelievingly. "It's a fool's dream, this kind of a swim."

"It's less work to go ahead than to turn back, now," broke in Joe, his teeth accompanying his words with the clatter of castanets.

"No; the wind and tide would be with us going back," objected Butts. "We could almost drift back."

"And die of chills on the way," contended Tom, doggedly. "No, sir! We've got to go ahead. I'm swimming to the tune of thoughts of the galley fire aboard the 'Restless'!"

"Br-r-r!" shook Hank, as the three cast loose from the log once more and struck out, panting, yet too cold to stay idle any longer.

It was tantalizing enough. The longer they swam, the more the boys began to believe that the island they sought was retreating from before them. Hank was almost certain they were moving in a circle, but Halstead, with a keen sense of location, insisted that they were going straight, even if very slowly, to the nameless island.

"I see it," breathed the young skipper, exultantly, at last.

"What—the island?" bellowed Hank Butts.

"No; but I'd swear I saw the 'Restless' the last time we rode a high wave," Halstead shouted back.

Ten minutes afterwards all three of the Motor Boat Club boys caught occasional glimpses of something dark and vague that they believed to be the hull of their yacht. The belief gave them renewed courage. Even Hank no longer had any desire to turn back. His whole thought centered on the lively times that were likely to begin when they tried to regain control of their boat from whomever had stolen it.

Then, bit by bit the trio worked their log buoy into the cove. Once they were inside, the water was very much smoother. Resting a few moments for breath, they then made a last dash forward, to get alongside.

In this smoother, more shallow water, the "Restless" rode securely at anchor. As they swam closer, the boys found that they could discover no human presence on the decks. Had the boat-stealers gone ashore on the nameless island? If so, it would be a comparatively easy matter to get aboard and cut out of the cove with their own craft.

Close up alongside they went. Tom Halstead was the first to be able to reach up at the hull and draw himself up over the side. Then, with his pocket-knife, as he lay at the rail of the "Restless," the young skipper slashed the cord that still held him bound to the log. Reaching over, he passed the knife to Hank. In utter silence the Long Island boy cut the clubs free, and passed them up. Next Hank drew himself aboard, after passing the jackknife to Joe Dawson.

Just a little later all three of the Motor Boat Club boys found themselves standing on the deck, each grasping his own firewood weapon. They made no noise, for they knew not who, or how many others might be on board below. If they had a desperate gang of thieves to contend with, then their troubles had not yet even begun!

Joe and Hank stood where they were, shaking as though in the last ditch of ague, while Halstead went forward, with the soft tread of a cat, to peer down into the motor room, the hatchway of which stood open.

"Wonder if there's anyone down there, asleep, or playing possum?" thought the young skipper as he peered into the blackness and listened. No sound of any kind came up to him. At last, a short step at a time, Halstead descended into the motor room, groping cautiously about. Finally, he became confident enough to feel in the galley match-box, extract a match and light it. The tiny flame showed him that the motor room was empty of human presence other than his own.

"No one down forward," he reported, in a shaking whisper, when he rejoined his chilled companions on deck.

"I believe there are plenty of folks in the cabin, though," reported Joe. "They've drawn the port-hole and transom curtains, but they've got a hidden light down there, and I can hear voices."

"Wait a moment, then," said Captain Tom, apprehensively. "I've an idea."

He crept back into the motor room, again striking a match. By the aid of this feeble light he found his way to the passageway that connected the motor room and the cabin under the bridge deck. After a brief inspection he hurried back to his comrades.

"The passage door is padlocked on the motor room side," he whispered. "Our pirates had no key to unlock that with. Now, can you walk the deck as though your shoes were soled with loose cotton?"

"Yes," grumbled Hank, disjointedly, "but the snare-drum solo my teeth are doing may make noise enough to give me away."

"Cram your handkerchief between your teeth," retorted Captain Tom, practically. "Come along, fellows. But hold your clubs ready in case your feet betray you."

Stealing along, each holding to the edge of the deck house with one hand, the motor boat boys approached the after hatchway. This, evidently for purposes of ventilation, had been left partly open.

Nudging his comrades to pause, Joe, bending so low as to be almost flat on the deck, prowled further aft.

There, in the darkness, he used his eyes to find out what might be down in the cabin. Then he came back.

"Eight tough-looking men in the cabin," he whispered, in Tom Halstead's ear.

"Is Anson Dalton one of them?"

"Yep."

"Hurrah! Then we've bagged him, at last!"

"Have we, though?" muttered Joe Dawson, dubiously.

"Well, we're going to," declared Tom, radiantly. "My boy, we're going to cut out of this cove with, the whole crew held in down there."

"Hope so," assented Joe, not very enthusiastically.

"Why, we've got to," argued Halstead. "If we don't, then that crew would have the upper hand, instead, and make penny jumping-jacks of us until they saw fit to let us go. But wait a moment. I must get back and have a look at them."

This time it was the young skipper who crawled aft. Joe and Hank followed part of the way, holding their sticks in readiness in case Dalton and his men discovered their presence.

"I reckon, Cap, you'll find you've got the right crowd for to-night's work," a rough voice was declaring, as Halstead came within ear range.

"Now, don't you men misunderstand me," replied Anson Dalton in a smooth yet firm voice. "I'm not paying you for any piratical acts. I have to give a little heed to the laws of the land, even if you fellows don't. What I want is this: At about two in the morning, when, most likely, everyone will be asleep except the one who is nursing the fellow Clodis, it is my plan to run in at Lonely Island's dock. We'll get quietly up to the house, suddenly force the door, and rush in. But, mind you all, there's to be no riot. Your numbers, and your rough appearance, will be enough to scare the folks of the bungalow. The two of you that I've already picked out will rush in with a stateroom door and one of the stateroom mattresses. With this for a stretcher, you two will get Clodis carefully and gently down to this boat. Then we'll sail away, and I'll tell you what to do next. But remember, no violent assault on anyone—no lawlessness, no hurting anyone badly. Trust to your numbers and suddenness. There's some baggage, too, in the bungalow, that I mean to bring away with me. I'll make off with it in the confusion."

"Oh, will you?" wondered Captain Tom Halstead, his jaw settling squarely.

Then, tiptoeing softly over to where Hank waited, the young skipper whispered something in that youth's ear. Hank fled quietly forward, but returned with a snap-padlock, the ring of which was open. With this in his hands Tom stole back aft, this time going close, indeed, to the hatchway.

"Hey! Someone on deck," roared an excited voice below.

There was an instant babel of voices, a rushing of feet and a general rumpus below. Two men in the van raced for the hatchway.

Slam! snap! click! Tom Halstead swung the hatchway door shut, forced the stout hasp over the staple and fastened the padlock in place!

CHAPTER VI
CARRYING DANGEROUS LIVE "FREIGHT"

"Cooped!" chuckled Joe Dawson, jubilantly.

Yet his voice could not much more than be heard above the racket that sounded below. Anson Dalton and his seven rough men were raising a hubbub, indeed.

"Smash the door down!" roared Dalton.

"Maybe we kin do it, boss, but the hatch is a stout one, and we ain't jest 'zactly fixed for tools," replied another voice.

After a few moments the fruitless hammering with mere fists subsided. In that time Hank Butts had raced forward, and now was back again with a prize that he had caught up from a locker near the motors. This was nothing more nor less than the hitching weight that Hank had once made very nearly famous, as described in the preceding volume, "THE MOTOR BOAT CLUB OFF LONG ISLAND."

"Let 'em get out if they can," advised Hank, grimly. "This for the feet, or the head, of the first roustabout that shows himself!"

Joe now raced forward to set the motors in motion. Though the young trio had temporary command of the deck, there was no telling how soon they would be overwhelmed. Every moment must be made to count.

Captain Tom, grasping his stick, stood by to help Hank in case the furious ones below succeeded in breaking out.

Hardly any time passed before the rhythmic chugging of the motors came to the young skipper's delighted ears. Then Joe waved his arms as a signal from the raised deck forward. Halstead swiftly joined his chum. Together they got the anchor up, stowing it well enough for the present.

"Now, you'd better get back to Hank, hadn't you?" quivered Joe. "I can handle speed and the wheel, too."

"Bless you, old Joe!" murmured Captain Tom, fervently, and raced aft. Dawson leaped to the wheel, at the same time setting one of the bridge controls so that the "Restless" began to move forward under slow speed. This move came just in time, for, even in the cove, the water had motion enough to threaten the yacht with grounding.

But now alert Joe Dawson swung the boat's head around, pointing her nose out of the cove.

"Get that hatch down in a hurry!" sounded Anson Dalton's hoarse voice, imperiously. "If you don't, we'll all be tight in a worse trap than this."

Blows with fists and feet resounded once more. Then, after an instant's pause, came the slower, harder thump-thump which told that one of the strongest of those caught below was using his shoulder, instead. Soon two cracks seamed the surface of the hatch door.

"Good! Go at it hard!" encouraged the voice of Dalton. "Batter it down. It will be worth money—and freedom—to you and to us all!"

"Yes, just clear a passage, and see what happens!" roared back Tom Halstead, as soon as he could make his own voice heard distinctly.

"Don't mind the talk of those boys!" warned Dalton, angrily, as there came a pause in the shoulder assaults against the hatch.

With a grin Hank raised his iron hitching weight above his head, hurling it down to the deck with crashing force. Then, still grinning, he stooped to pick it up again.

That noisy thump on the deck timbers caused a brief ensuing silence down in the cabin. It was plain that Dalton and his fellows were wondering just how dangerous their reception would be in case they succeeded in breaking out.

The cabin was lighted, in day time, by side ports and a barred transom overhead. The ports were too small to permit of a man forcing his way through. Even though they broke the glass overhead, the prisoners in the cabin would still have iron bars to overcome. Tom Halstead, with his club, could hinder any work at that point.

In the meantime, the "Restless," once out of the cove, was bounding over the waves like a thing of life. Though the water had been hard to swim through, it did not present a rough sea for a fifty-five foot power boat.

In less than three minutes Engineer Joe Dawson was sounding his auto whistle like mad as he neared the dock at Lonely Island.

Just as the boat glided in, under decreased headway, to the dock the bungalow door was seen to open. Powell Seaton, shot-gun in hand, appeared on the porch. He watched, not knowing whether friend or foe commanded the "Restless." Mr. Seaton, himself, was made to stand out brightly in the middle of the searchlight ray that Joe turned upon him, yet he could not see who was behind that light.

Running the boat in, bow-on, Joe leaped ashore with the hawser. Making fast only at the bow, he next raced up the board walk, shouting the news to Mr.

Seaton. The latter, with a hail of delight, darted toward the dock, arriving barely behind Dawson.

Down in the cabin the din of the men trying to escape had redoubled. Powell Seaton tramped hurriedly aft, while Tom and Joe fell in behind him with heavy tread, to give the rascals below an idea that numerous reinforcements had arrived.

Bang! Pausing before the hatch Mr. Seaton raised the shot-gun to his shoulder, discharging a single shell. Hastily slipping one into the magazine of the weapon to replace the fired one, Seaton shouted sternly:

"Stop your nonsense down there! If you get out it will be only to run into the muzzles of fire-arms. You fellows are fairly caught!"

There was a startled silence, followed by indistinct mutterings. Not even Anson Dalton, it appeared, cared to brave what looked like too certain death.

Tom held a whispered consultation with his employer, then stepped over to young Butts.

"Hank, we're going to leave you on shore. Mr. Seaton will come along with the gun. Keep your eyes open—until you see us again! Don't be caught napping. Remember, you and Dr. Cosgrove have the whole protection of that helpless man, Clodis, *in* your hands."

Hank Butts made a wry face for a moment. He would have much preferred to see the present adventure through. Yet, a second later, the Long Island boy bounded to the dock, then stood to cast off the bow-line.

After the line had come aboard, Joe Dawson again took his place at the wheel, turning on the speed gradually as the boat rounded out past the island, then turned in toward the mainland.

It was about five miles, in a direct westerly course, to the shore, but by an oblique, northwesterly course a fishing village some nine miles away could be reached.

"Steer for the fishing village," nodded Powell Seaton. Captain Tom hurried forward to give the order, adding: "Make it at full speed, Joe. If you have to go to the engine, call me forward to take the wheel."

Soon afterwards Tom slipped into the motor room, rubbed down and got on dry clothing. Joe, in turn, did likewise, afterward returning to the wheel.

Down in the cabin all had been quiet for some minutes after the discharge of the gun on deck. Yet Captain Tom, by peeping through the transom, discovered the heads of Dalton and some of his rough men close together in consultation.

"I'll annoy them a bit," chuckled the young skipper, moving swiftly forward. Dropping down into the motor room he switched off all the cabin lights. An instant roar of anger came from below.

"Funny we didn't think of that before," grinned Dawson, as Halstead came up out of the motor room.

"It'll bother the rascals a bit," chuckled Captain Tom back over his shoulder.

With such a boat as the "Restless" ordinary distances are swiftly covered. It was barely twenty-five minutes after leaving the dock that Joe reached the entrance to the little harbor around which the houses of the fishing village clustered, nor had much speed been used.

Now the whistle sounded steadily, in short, sharp blasts. Moreover, Dawson managed to send the distress signal with the searchlight. By the time he slowed down speed, then reversed, to make the little wharf, a dozen men had hurried down to the shore.

"What's wrong?" hailed one of them.

"Get the sheriff, or a sheriff's officer!" shouted back Powell Seaton. "Be quick about it, one of you, please, and the rest of you stay here to help us."

Joe sent the bow hawser flying ashore, Tom doing the same with the stern line. Willing hands caught both ropes, making them fast around snubbing posts. As two men started away on the run, the rest of the bystanders came crowding aboard, filled with curiosity.

"What happens to be wrong on board?" demanded one bronzed fisherman.

"We've a cabin full of pirates, or rascals about as bad," returned Mr. Seaton, grimly.

"Men of this coast?" asked another speaker.

"Yes, evidently," nodded Mr. Seaton, whom the new-comers had recognized as the owner of Lonely Island.

"Then they must be the crew of the 'Black Betty,'" commented the first speaker.

"Is that a black, fifty-foot schooner, low in the water, narrow and carrying tall masts with a heavy spread of canvas?" interposed Tom Halstead.

"Yes," nodded the fisherman. "That's the 'Black Betty.' She claims to be a fishing boat, but we're ready to bet she's a smuggler. She carries nine men, including Captain Dave Lemly."

"I reckon we've got most of the 'Black Betty' outfit below, then," declared Captain Halstead. "Or else—gracious!"

For, at that moment, the cracked hatch gave in with a smash. Powell Seaton had neglected to remain on guard closely. There was a surge of the prisoners below.

"Halstead, you'll hear from me again—and so will your crew!" shouted Anson Dalton out of the press of struggling men that formed on the after deck. "I won't let you forget me, Halstead!"

There was a splash past the rail. Dalton had gone overboard, followed by two of his companions.

CHAPTER VII
POWELL SEATON'S BAD CASE OF "FORGET"

"Don't let any more get away!" called Powell Seaton, excitedly.

Tom Halstead promptly leaped at one of the rough fugitives just as the latter was trying to reach the wharf. Another one Joe Dawson grabbed. Several of the fishermen sprang to help. For a minute or two there was a good deal of confusion. When matters quieted down, it was found that Halstead and Dawson, with the fishermen helping, had secured five of the rough lot.

Powell Seaton, by threatening with his shot-gun, had induced a sixth to swim ashore. But Anson Dalton and another man, believed to be Captain Dave Lemly of the "Black Betty," had escaped, swimming under water in the darkness. They must have come to the surface at some point not far away, yet, in the black darkness of the night, they managed to escape safely for the time being, at any rate.

The six men thus arrested were forced inside a ring of the fishermen, whose numbers had been greatly increased by new arrivals. Powell Seaton, his shot-gun on his shoulder, now patrolled close to the human ring. Three or four men hurried with Tom and Joe on a quest for Anson Dalton and the latter's companion in flight.

In less than a quarter of an hour one of the messengers who had first hurried away returned with a deputy sheriff, who brought several pairs of handcuffs. A justice of the peace was aroused at his home, and held the prisoners over for trial, after Powell Seaton had preferred against them a charge of stealing the yacht that was under his charter.

The search for Dalton and his companion was given up, for it became plain that both had succeeded in their effort to get away.

"It's altogether too bad," sighed Mr. Seaton, on coming out of the justice's house. "However, we can be thankful for what success we have had. We have the boat back and have balked Dalton's rascals in what they were planning for to-night."

"Are you going back to Lonely Island now, sir?" asked Captain Tom.

"We must, very soon," replied Mr. Seaton. "Yet, Halstead, I've been thinking that I cannot afford to take any further chances, with Anson Dalton still at large. These fishermen are a rough but honest lot of splendid fellows in their way. I'm going to see if I can't hire a special guard of eight men for Lonely Island for the present. I'll engage the deputy sheriff to vouch for the men I engage. So go down to the boat and be ready for me as soon as I arrive."

Joe was aboard, waiting, when the young skipper returned. Several of the men of the village were still about the dock.

"We're to be ready to cast off as soon as Mr. Seaton gets here, Joe," Captain Tom Halstead announced. "Better look to your motors. If you want any help, call on me."

It did not take Mr. Seaton very long to recruit the guard of eight men that he wanted. Carrying rifles or shot-guns, borrowed in some instances, the men tramped along after their new employer. They came aboard, two or three of them going below, the others preferring to remain on deck.

"Cast off, Captain, as soon as you can," directed Powell Seaton.

Two or three of the new guards sprang forward to help in this work. Halstead rang for half speed, then threw the wheel over, making a quick start. Once under way, he called for full speed, and the "Restless" went bounding over the waves, which were running much lower than a couple of hours earlier.

During the first half of the run Captain Halstead remained at the wheel. Then Joe came up from below, relieving him. Tom strolled back to take a seat on the deck-house beside Mr. Seaton.

"I'm on tenterhooks to get back," confessed the charter-man.

"Anxious about your friend, Clodis, of course," nodded Tom, understandingly.

"Partly that, yes. But there's another matter that's bothering me fearfully, too. You remember the packet of papers I took from Clodis's trunk?" asked Mr. Seaton, lowering his voice.

"Yes," murmured Tom. "But you have those in an inner pocket."

"I wish I had!" uttered Powell Seaton. "Halstead, the truth is, after you young men went out, this evening, to patrol about the island, I became a little uneasy about that packet, and took it out and hid it—under some boxes of ammunition in the cupboard where I keep my gun. Then I locked the closet door. When Dawson called me from the porch, in such haste, and I was needed on board with my gun, I clean forgot the packet for the instant."

"Oh, it will be safe, anyway," Tom assured his employer. "Even if Dalton had been able to get a boat at once, in this neighborhood, there's no other craft in these waters capable of reaching Lonely Island earlier than we shall do it."

"I *do* hope that packet is safe," muttered Mr. Seaton, in a voice tense with anxiety. "Halstead, you've no notion of the fearful blow it would be to friends and to myself to have it disappear."

Hearing a slight noise on the opposite side of the deck-house top, Seaton and Tom Halstead turned together. They were just in time to see one of the new guards leaning toward them, one hand out as though to steady himself.

"It's rough footing on deck to-night," said the guard, with a pleasant laugh, then passed on aft.

Tom took the helm again as the "Restless," after picking up the landing place with the searchlight, moved into the harbor and went to her berth.

Powell Seaton led all of his guards but one up to the bungalow. The eighth man, armed with a rifle, was left aboard the "Restless," with the searchlight turned on, ready for use at any moment. Tom and Joe went up to the bungalow with their employer.

"Wait out on the porch for just a little while," called Mr. Seaton, in a low voice. "And be careful to make no noise that will disturb the sick man."

Five minutes later Mr. Seaton returned to the porch.

"I've been looking for that packet," he whispered to the young skipper. "It's safe, so I've left it in the same place."

Then, after a moment, the owner of the bungalow added:

"Captain, you can have your friend, Butts, now, as we can do without him in the house. I think you three had better turn in on the boat and get some sleep. Then, soon after daylight, I can have the guard at the wharf rouse you, for I want you to go over to Beaufort and get supplies for repairing the wireless outfit at the earliest hour. Things are likely to happen soon that will make it dangerous for me to be without wireless communication with land and sea."

Twenty minutes later the three Motor Boat Club boys were stretched out in their berths in the motor room. It was considerably later, though, ere sleep came to them. When slumber did reach their eyes they slept soundly until called by the guard.

Hank prepared a breakfast in record time. After eating this, and after Hank had been sent up to the house to learn whether there were any further orders, the Motor Boat Club boys were ready to cast off.

Once they were under way, Hank, not being needed, went aft to stretch himself on one of the cabin cushions. Joe, having his motors running smoothly, followed Hank into the cabin. Dawson, however, did not seek further sleep. He wanted to make a more thorough test than he had done a few hours before, in order to make sure that the vandals locked in there the night before had not thought to destroy his beloved wireless instruments or connections.

"The whole wireless plant is in shape for instant use," he reported, coming back at last to the bridge deck.

"That's mighty good news," declared Tom Halstead. "With the man we are working for now we're likely to need the wireless at any minute in the twenty-four hours."

"Say," ejaculated Joe, after a few moments of silent thought, "there's something hugely mysterious and uncanny back of all these doings of less than twenty-four hours. I wonder what that big mystery really is?"

CHAPTER VIII
THE RED MESSAGE

When the boys reached Beaufort and had tied up at a wharf, it was still too early to expect to find any shops open. They left Hank on watch, however, and went up into the town, Joe to look, presently, for a dealer in electrical supplies, while Captain Tom sought a ship's joiner to fit and hang a new hatch to replace that smashed in the affair of the night before. Both boys were presently successful, though it was noon before the joiner had his task finished.

While the last of the work on the new hatch was being done, Tom and Joe went once more uptown to get a message from Mr. Seaton's attorney regarding the date when the formal hearing of the men arrested the night before would take place in court. Hank Butts was left to watch over the boat and keep an eye over the joiner.

"Any strangers around here?" queried the young skipper, after the joiner, his work completed, had gone aboard.

"Only a young black boy," Hank replied. "He seemed curious to look over the boat, but he didn't offer to go below, or touch anything, so I didn't chase him off."

"Cast off, Hank. Give us some power, Joe, and we'll get back to Lonely Island," declared the young captain, going to the wheel.

Hardly more than a minute later the "Restless" was gliding out of the harbor.

"Guess Hank's young negro visitor left a note," called up Joe, showing in the doorway of the motor room and holding forth a note. Hank took it, passing it to Halstead.

"Mind the wheel a minute, Hank, please," requested Tom, looking closely at the envelope.

It was addressed only to "Halstead," the writing being in red, and thick, as though laid on with the point of a stick. The message on the sheet inside was crisp and to the point. It ran:

If you think your doings have been forgotten, you'll soon know differently!

"Humph!" muttered Joe, following up, and taking the sheet as his chum held it out. "That must be from Anson Dalton."

"Or Captain Dave Lemly, of the 'Black Betty,'" returned Tom, without a trace of concern in his tone.

"It's a threat, all right," muttered Hank Butts, his hair bristling when the sheet came into his hands. "Confound 'em, I hope whoever sent this tries to make good—when we're looking!"

Just then Captain Tom changed the course abruptly, the bows of the "Restless" sending up a shower of spray that sprinkled Hank from head to foot. As he turned to get out of the way the wind caught the sheet written in red from his hand, blowing it out across the water.

"Let it go," laughed Tom. "We know all the red message had to say."

"The negro that I allowed on deck came on purpose to drop the note where it would be found," muttered Hank.

"No matter," smiled Tom. "We're always glad to know that we're remembered by nice people."

"I'd like to have that black boy here for a minute or two," grunted Hank, clenching his fists.

"What for?" Tom Halstead queried. "He probably didn't have any guilty knowledge about the sender."

"That reminds me," broke in Joe. "Stand close by the motors a few minutes, will you, Hank?"

With that Dawson vanished aft. When he came back he announced:

"I've just flashed the wireless word back to Mr. Seaton's lawyer about the message we got, advising the lawyer that it probably shows Dalton, or Lemly, or both, to be in Beaufort. And the lawyer was able to send me news, received just after we left."

"What?"

"The schooner, 'Black Betty,' has just been seized, thirty miles down the coast, by United States officers. She'll be held until the customs men have had a chance to look into the charges that the schooner has been used in the smuggling trade."

"Was Lemly caught with her?" asked Tom, eagerly.

"No such luck," retorted Joe.

"I'd feel better over hearing that Dave Lemly was the prisoner of the United States Government," remarked young Halstead. "If he keeps at liberty *he* is the one who is going to be able to make Anson Dalton dangerous to us."

"Then you're beginning to be afraid of that pair, are you?" asked Joe Dawson, looking up.

"No, I'm not," rejoined Tom Halstead, his jaws firmly set. "A man—or a boy, either for that matter—who can be made afraid of other people isn't fit to be trusted with the command of a boat on the high seas. But I'll say this much about my belief concerning Dalton: For some reason we've been in his way, and are likely to be much more in his way before we're through with him. If Dalton got a chance, he wouldn't hesitate to wreck the 'Restless,' or to blow her up. For any work of that sort Dave Lemly is undoubtedly his man."

"What can make them so desperate against Mr. Seaton?" queried Joe.

"We can't even guess, for we don't yet know the story that's behind all this mystery and the list of desperate deeds."

"I wonder if Mr. Seaton will ever tell us?" pondered Joe.

"Not unless he thinks we really need to know."

"But he has already hinted that it's all in a big fight for a fortune," urged Hank.

"Yes, and we can guess that the fight centers in South America, since that is where Clodis was bound for when this business started," replied Skipper Tom.

"I wonder if there's any chance that our cruise will reach to South America?" broke in Hank Butts, eagerly.

"Hardly likely," replied Tom, with a shake of the head. "If there had been even a chance of that, Mr. Seaton would have arranged for an option extending beyond the end of this month."

"Just my luck," grumbled Hank, seating himself on the edge of the deck-house. "Nothing big ever happens to me."

"Say, you're hard to please," laughed Joe, turning and going down into the motor room.

They were not long in making Lonely Island, where the "Restless" was tied up and the hatchways locked securely. The boys were not required to remain at the boat, one of the guards being stationed, night or day, at the wharf.

Powell Seaton was much interested in the account Tom gave him of the red message, though he did not say much.

There was no change or improvement in the condition of Mr. Clodis, who still lay in a darkened room, like one dead.

That afternoon Joe, with some help from his comrades, repaired the bungalow's wireless plant and got in touch with the shore once more.

Through the night four men were kept on guard, one on the porch, another at the wharf, and two others patrolling the island. No attempt of any sort on the part of Dalton or the latter's confederates was discovered.

The next morning brought still no change in the condition of Clodis. He was alive, breathing feebly, and Dr. Cosgrove was attempting to ward off an attack of brain fever.

Through the forenoon Joe was kept rather busy sending messages ashore to the authorities, for Powell Seaton, though not leaving the island, was waging a determined campaign to get hold of Dalton.

"I don't need Dalton, particularly," confessed Mr. Seaton, as he sat with the three motor boat boys at the noon meal. "But it would be worth a very great deal of money to get back the papers that Dalton must have stolen after assaulting my sick friend, yonder, on board the 'Constant.'"

"Do you—do you know—what was in the stolen papers?" asked Captain Tom Halstead, hesitatingly.

"Very well, indeed," rejoined their employer, with emphasis. "But the real trouble is that I don't want to have that knowledge pass to the gang that are behind Anson Dalton."

"Yet Dalton must have had time to join his principals, or confederates, by this time, and turn the papers over to them," hazarded Halstead.

"That's hardly likely," murmured Powell Seaton, "since the gang of rascals behind Anson Dalton must be, at this moment, somewhere in the interior of Brazil."

"Oh!" said Tom, reflectively.

"You're curious, I see, to know what all this great mystery means," smiled Mr. Seaton.

"I—I don't want to let myself be curious about what is none of my business," declared Tom Halstead, bluntly.

"I'm going to tell you the story now, just the same," replied Powell Seaton, in a still lower voice.

CHAPTER IX
MR. SEATON UNBURDENS HIMSELF

"Really, I see no reason why I shouldn't tell you," went on the charter-man of the "Restless." "When I first engaged you youngsters and your boat for this month I had little more in mind than using your boat for pleasure cruising about here. Yet the fact that you had a wireless equipment aboard the 'Restless' *did* influence me not a little, for I had at least a suspicion that big affairs might come to pass, and that telegraphing from ship to ship might be wonderfully convenient.

"At the same time, I was careful to look up the references that you gave me, Captain Halstead. Those references were so wholly satisfactory that I know I can trust you to serve me as bravely and loyally as you have, in the past, been called upon to serve others. And now, just for the reason that you may be called upon to take some big fighting chances for me, I'm going to tell you what lies back of the curtain of mystery that you've been staring at."

As his voice died out Powell Seaton arose, locked the door and glanced out through the windows. Then he returned to the table, motioning to the boys to incline their heads close to his.

"Probably," began their host, "you've regarded me as a wealthy man, and, until the last two or three days, as one of leisure. I am reasonably well-to-do in this world's goods, but most of my life, since I was twenty, has been passed in storm and stress.

"It is not necessary to tell you all about the life that I have led. It will be enough to tell you that, three years ago, not satisfied that my fortune was large enough, I went to Brazil in order to learn what chance there might be of picking up money fast in that country.

"In Brazil there are many ways of making a fortune, though perhaps not as many as right here at home. However, there are fewer fortune-seekers there. In coffee, rubber and in many other staples fortunes may be made in Brazil, but the biggest, wildest, most desperate and scrambling gamble of all is found in the diamond-digging fields.

"Most of the diamond fields have, perhaps, been discovered, and their working has become systematized to a regular, dividend-paying basis. There are still,

however, some fields not yet located. It was a small field, but one which I
believe may be worth millions, that I located somewhat more than a year ago.
See here!"

From an inner pocket Powell Seaton drew forth an ordinary wallet. Opening it,
he dropped out on the table six diamonds. Though none was of great size, all of
the stones were of such purity and such flashing brilliancy that the motor boat
boys gazed at them in fascination.

"They must be worth a fortune," declared Hank Butts, in an awed, subdued
tone.

"Not exactly," smiled Mr. Seaton. "These stones have been appraised, I
believe, at about twelve thousand dollars."

After passing the gems from hand to hand, the owner of the bungalow replaced
them in the wallet, returning the latter to the same pocket before he resumed:

"This new diamond field, a patent to which has not yet been filed with the
Brazilian Government, is in the state of Vahia. There is no harm in telling
anyone that, as Vahia is a state of great area. It is in a section little likely to be
suspected as a diamond field, and the chance that someone else will accidentally
discover and locate it is not large."

"Yet you know the exact location—can go right to it?" breathed Tom
Halstead, his eyes turned squarely on Mr. Seaton's.

"Yes, but I don't dare go to it," came the smiling answer.

"Oh! May I ask why not, sir?"

"The Government of Brazil is, in the main, an honest one," replied Powell
Seaton. "The President of that country is an exactly just and honorable man. Yet
not quite as much can be said for the governments of *some* of the states of that
country. The governor of Vahia, Terrero, by name, is probably one of the worst
little despots in South America.

"Now, as it happened, before I came to know anything about this new
diamond field I had the bad fortune to make an enemy of Governor Terrero.
Some American friends were being shamefully treated by this rascally governor,
and I felt called upon to become mixed up in the affair. I even went so far that I
incurred the deadly hatred of Terrero. It was right after this that I came upon my
diamond field. But Terrero's enmity was pressing upon me, and I had to flee
from Brazil."

"Why?" asked Tom, wonderingly.

"Do you know how things are done in South America?" demanded Powell
Seaton, impressively. "If a man like Terrero hates you, he has only to inspire
someone to prefer a serious charge against you. The charge may be wholly false,
of course, but officers and soldiers are sent, in the dead of the night, to arrest
you. These wretches, when they serve wicked enough officials, shoot you down
in cold blood. Then they lay beside your body a revolver in which are two or
three discharged cartridges. They report, officially, that you resisted arrest and
did your best to kill the members of the arresting party. This infamous lie all
becomes a matter of official record. Then what can the United States
Government do about it? And the governor, or other rascally official, has
triumphed over you, and the matter is closed. Though an honest man, Halstead,

you are officially a desperate character who *had* to be killed by the law's servants. It was such a fate that Terrero was preparing for me, but I escaped his wicked designs."

"That must be a nice country!" murmured Hank Butts.

"Yet you say the President of Brazil is an honorable man?" asked Halstead. "Can't he remove such a governor?"

"The President would, in a moment, if he could be supplied with proofs," rejoined Powell Seaton, with emphasis. "Governor Terrero is a wily, smooth scoundrel who is well served by men of his own choice stamp. Terrero is wealthy, and backed by many other wealthy men who have been growing rich in the diamond fields. In fact, though they are wonderfully smooth about it, the Terrero gang are terrors to all honest diamond men in that one part of Brazil."

"So, then," hinted Captain Tom, "you know where to find one of the rich diamond mines of the world, but you don't dare go to it?"

"I'd dare," retorted Mr. Seaton, his eyes flashing. "But what would be the use of daring? I am almost certain to be killed if I ever show my face in Vahia while Terrero is alive. So, then, this is what I have done: Since my return to this country I have been arranging, ever so quietly, with moneyed men who have faith in me and in my honesty. After much dickering we have arranged a syndicate that is backed by millions of dollars, if need be. And we may need to spend a good deal of money before we get through. We may even have to try to turn Terrero's most trusted lieutenants against him. We won't, if we can help it, but we may have to. The stake is a big one!

"Through turning this business over to the syndicate I am bound to lose the greater portion of the fortune that might have been mine from this great enterprise. Yet, even as it is, I stand to reap rich returns if ever the syndicate can locate and secure the patent to the diamond fields that I discovered.

"At this moment three members of our syndicate are in Rio Janeiro. They are big, solid American men of moneyed affairs. As far as they permit to be known, they are in Brazil only as a matter of vacation and pleasure. In truth, they are awaiting the arrival of Albert Clodis on the 'Constant.' When he had arrived, with the papers from me showing where and how to locate the diamond field, they were to have moved quickly, spending plenty of money, and filing a patent to the fields. Under the law the Brazilian Government would be entitled to a large share of the find in precious stones, but even at that our share would have been enormous. Once the patent to the diamond field was filed, the President and the whole National Government of that country could be depended upon to protect the owner's rights, even against the greed and treachery of Terrero. So all that appeared to be left to do was to get to my friends of the syndicate the two sets of papers that would enable them to locate the unknown diamond field. Neither set of papers is worth anything by itself, but with the two sets the field can be promptly located.

"My first thought was to send the two sets of papers by two different men. Yet, strange as it may appear to you boys, I could not decide upon two men whom I felt I could fully trust under all circumstances. You have no idea how I have been watched, the last year, by agents of Terrero. Dalton, though an

American, is one of the worst of these secret agents of the governor of Vahia. *I knew how thoroughly I was being watched, and I, in turn, have had others watching Anson Dalton* as effectively as it could be done in a free country like the United States.

"Well, to make this long story short, when I had all else in readiness I decided upon Bert Clodis as the one man I could fully trust to deliver the two sets of papers to the members of the syndicate at Rio Janeiro. I believed, too, at the time, though I could not be sure, that my relations with Bert Clodis were unknown to Anson Dalton.

"Yet, not for a moment did I trust too thoroughly to that belief. I had Dalton watched. If he engaged passage aboard the 'Constant,' my suspicions would be at once aroused. We now know that he secured passage, by mail, under the name of Arthur Hilton. Beyond the slightest doubt Dalton, that infernal spy, had succeeded in discovering that I was sending Clodis with the papers. Yet Dalton, or Hilton, as he chose to call himself, did not go aboard the 'Constant' openly at New York. I can only guess that he boarded from the tug that took off the pilot when the liner had reached open sea.

"I had impressed upon Bert Clodis the importance of keeping the two sets of papers apart, and had advised him that it might not be safe to deposit either in the purser's safe, from which they might be taken through the means of a deep-sea burglary.

"So the probability is that Bert Clodis had one set of papers concealed on his person. The other set of papers—the one I now have safe—he seems to have put away in his trunk, believing that no one seeking to rob him would think him simple enough to leave valuable papers in a trunk that could be rather easily entered in the hold of a liner.

"As I have already told you, I had the ship watched at New York, and received a message, after her sailing, which told me that no one answering Dalton's description had boarded the 'Constant' at her pier.

"As the liner entered this latitude Bert Clodis was to send off a wireless message which, though apparently rather blind, would be enough to advise me that no one answering to Dalton's description had appeared among the passengers or crew of the 'Constant.' This news I awaited at the wireless station at Beaufort, and you can imagine my anxiety."

"That was why, then," broke in Joe, suddenly, "when I received that message about the injury to Mr. Clodis, you were able to break in so quickly?"

"Yes," nodded Mr. Seaton. "I was waiting, and was on tenterhooks. I would have joined you, and would have gone out in haste to receive Bert Clodis myself, but I realized that, if I delayed you, the big liner would get past us, and Bert Clodis must most likely die on the way to Brazil."

"Why weren't you out here, sir, at this bungalow, where you could have received the message as well, and then have gone out with us on the 'Restless'?" inquired Tom Halstead, with deepest interest in this strange narration.

"I was at Beaufort," responded Mr. Seaton, "because I felt it very necessary to be where I could use a private wire to New York that I had reserved. I was, at that time, waiting for word from New York of any possible discovery that could be made concerning the movements of the infamous Dalton, whom I did not then know, or believe, to be on board the 'Constant.'"

There was silence for a few moments, but Powell Seaton at last went on, thoughtfully:

"We now know that Bert Clodis did *not* deposit any papers with the purser of the ship. One set of the papers, therefore, must have been tucked away in his clothing. Dalton, after assaulting Bert Clodis, or having it done, must have rifled his pockets and found one set. He even had time to look through them and discover that that set was incomplete. Then, on seeing Clodis's trunk go aboard the 'Restless' with the injured man, Dalton guessed that the remaining papers might be in the trunk. That was why Dalton decided to leave the 'Constant.' But your flat refusal to let him go down into the cabin, where the baggage had been taken, foiled the fellow at that point. Then, fearing that he would run into me, and that I might even resort to violence, Dalton hailed that schooner, the 'Black Betty,' and made his momentary escape."

"No doubt," interposed Halstead, "Dalton has had plenty of chance to put *his* set of the stolen papers in safe hiding. But isn't it barely likely that he had already engaged Captain Dave Lemly to be hanging about in these waters with that little black schooner?"

"Wholly likely," nodded Mr. Seaton, thoughtfully. "However, boys, I have trusted you with as much as my very life is worth in telling you all this. I would rather lose my life than see my friends, as well as myself, beaten in this great diamond game. As the matter now stands, Dalton has won the first step, but he hasn't enough knowledge to enable his employer, Terrero, to locate my precious find. I can duplicate the missing papers, and the other set, which I have here secure, I must also send to Rio Janeiro by some other most trusted messenger, should Clodis, poor fellow, die, or prove unfit to make another attempt."

"And do you think, sir, that there's only one honest man on earth?" asked Tom Halstead, in considerable surprise.

"There are several men that I *believe* to be honest," returned the owner of the bungalow, "yet only one that I know to be *honest*, and who possesses at the same time the judgment to undertake a mission like the one I have been telling you about."

"Then it won't really do Dalton any good to start for Brazil unless he can get hold of the contents of the other set of papers?" Halstead asked, after a pause of a few moments.

"Not until the fellow can get his clutches on the papers that I have secretly locked in that closet over there," confirmed Mr. Seaton. "And I have told none but you trustworthy youngsters that the other set *is* hidden in such an easy place to get at."

Then, as though struck by a thought, Powell Seaton crossed the room, drawing his key-ring from a pocket. He fitted the right key to the door, and swung the latter open. An instant more, and there came from Mr. Seaton's lips a cry much like the frightened howl of a wild beast.

"The second set of papers is gone—stolen from here!"

There was an almost simultaneous gasp of consternation from the three Motor Boat Club boys as they rushed forward. But they had no need to search. Seaton had done that thoroughly, and now he turned to eye them. As he stared—or glared—a new thought came into Seaton's mind, reflecting itself in his eyes. The boys could see him fighting against his own new suspicion.

"Halstead," cried Powell Seaton, clutching at the side of the doorway, "I told you all about this hiding place. I trusted you!"

It was Tom Halstead's turn to go deathly white and stagger.

"Do you mean, sir, that YOU SUSPECT ME?" demanded the young skipper, in a voice choked with horror.

CHAPTER X
THE TRAITOR AT THE AERIALS

"Wait! Don't take anything too seriously. I've—got to—think!"

Powell Seaton had stood, for two or three moments, staring from Halstead to the other motor boat boys.

"Humph! Well, this is good, but I don't like it," grimaced Hank Butts, taking two steps backward.

Powell Seaton began to pace the room, his hands at his head. He looked like one who suddenly found it impossible to think.

Hank opened his mouth to say something angry, but Captain Tom checked him with a look and a gesture.

"May we search in that closet for you, sir?" called Halstead, when a thud told that the owner of the bungalow had dropped heavily back into his chair.

"You may look there, if you want to. Anyone may look there—now!" uttered the amazed one.

Without saying more Tom, in deep agitation, began the task he had invited upon himself. Joe Dawson came and stood looking quietly over his chum's shoulder, ready to help if necessary. As for Hank, he stood, a picture of injured pride, staring at the distracted man.

"No; there's nothing here," admitted Halstead, at last. "At least, the only thing we're interested in isn't here."

"Of course it isn't," moaned Seaton. "Yet you boys were the only ones I told. And, the only time I left the house, it was safe upon my return. I also told you boys that."

"If he keeps on talking in that strain," muttered Hank, half-aloud, "I'll make his head ache!"

"No, you won't," uttered Captain Tom, gripping his comrade's arm almost fiercely. "There's trouble enough on the premises as it is. Hold your tongue, Hank, until we're all in a good mood to say pleasant things."

Thereupon, with a snort, Hank dragged a chair into a far corner, and seated himself in it.

Halstead walked slowly to the table, on which Mr. Seaton was resting his elbows, his face buried in his hands.

"There must be some explanation for this, Mr. Seaton," began the young motor boat skipper, more calmly. "I don't mind your first suspicion of me, because—"

"Not you, more than the others," broke in the bungalow's owner, excitedly. "All of you young men knew about the hiding-place. You were the only ones besides myself who did know."

Again Hank gripped his fists tightly, but a stern look from Joe Dawson prevented Butts from giving any further expression of his feelings.

"Don't sit there like that, Mr. Seaton," broke in Tom Halstead, once more. "Whatever has happened, something must be done—and it must be the right thing, and at once."

"You can search us, if you want—" began Hank's growling voice, but Joe Dawson stood before him, towering in grim purpose.

"Don't you open your mouth again, Hank, until you've collected some sense," warned Joe. "Let Tom do the talking. He's the captain, anyway."

"You're right," responded Powell Seaton, looking up in a good deal of a daze. "I must do something—quickly—yet what?"

"If anyone has stolen the final set of papers," advanced the young skipper, "it must have been either Dalton or someone working for him. In either case, Dalton must now have the papers, or he soon will have."

"But what does this lead to?" inquired Mr. Seaton, regarding his young captain dubiously.

"Why, sir, it must be plain that the best course is to drop all other steps and concentrate every bit of your energy and ingenuity on getting hold of Anson Dalton."

"Yet what can I do to him, if I do?"

"In the first place, you might charge him with being the man who struck Albert Clodis over the head. That would be enough to have your man arrested on, even if you couldn't prove the charge. A charge that you *can* fight on is that of having helped to steal the 'Restless' the other night. If you can only get the fellow locked up, then you'll have more time to find out whether there's any way of getting the missing papers away from him, or from any hiding place in which he has put them."

"Lock the fellow up?" jeered Powell Seaton. "Bah, boy, you don't seem to realize the money that's behind him. Ten thousand dollars, or a hundred thousand, it would all be the same, and Dalton, out on bail, could flee in whatever direction he wanted to."

"Then what *are* you going to do?" demanded Captain Tom, incisively.

In this instant of utter uncertainty a tinkling of a bell broke in upon them. It was the call bell that Dawson had attached to the wireless apparatus.

"Remember, *you* keep quiet," almost whispered Joe to Hank, then quitted the room hastily. Butts suddenly began to grin sheepishly. Rising, he sauntered over to a window.

Joe had hurried to the wireless room on the mere chance that it might be a message for Lonely Island. It was much more likely to be the regular business of ships passing on the sea. But as he entered the room Dawson heard the clicking call from a receiving instrument:

"CBA! CBA!" That was Lonely Island's call surely enough.

Breaking in at the key, Joe sent the sparks chasing each other up the aerials. Having answered, he slipped on the head-band, fitting the watch-case receivers over his ears. Picking up a pencil, he wrote.

It was a rush telegram from Mr. Seaton's lawyer, up at Beaufort, and it read:

Man much resembles description of Dalton has just been reported embarking on seventy-foot cruising motor boat ten miles above this city. Man in command of boat positively said to be Captain Dave Lemly.

"Remain at wire for further talk," Joe's trembling fingers signaled back. Then, leaping up, he bounded into the next room.

"Read it to me," Powell Seaton begged.

Tom Halstead took the sheet, reading rapidly yet clearly. The young skipper was excited, though he forced himself to remain cool.

"There's your call to action, Mr. Seaton," he wound up with.

"Yes, but what action?" demanded the owner of the bungalow. Ever since the discovery of the loss of the papers this man had seemed all but unable to speak.

"We've got to overhaul that other motor boat, though her length will have to be description enough if we can't get a better one," declared the young skipper. "Hank, go down and open up the motor room. Start the motors going, though be gentle. Don't break anything, or put the motors out of business. Joe, go back to the wireless, and see whether you can get a more exact description of that boat—especially the course she is believed to have sailed on. Hustle! Mr. Seaton, hadn't you better inform Dr. Cosgrove that you'll be absent for a while?"

The owner of the bungalow moved as though glad of directions that saved him the trouble of thinking.

Joe promptly sent a wireless back to Beaufort asking for a better description of the seventy-footer and the last course upon which she had been seen.

The only further word the lawyer's informant could furnish, as Joe ascertained ten minutes later, was that the boat was painted a drab tint and had a "smoke-stack" ventilator. When last seen the boat was heading out nearly due east from her starting-point.

"Going out to meet a liner, for some port," clicked Tom, as he heard the news. "Well, it's our business to find that drab motor boat."

As Joe caught up his cap, Mr. Seaton looked rather uncertainly from one boy to the other.

"You say we're to go out on this jaunt over the water," remarked the owner of the bungalow. "But I don't know. Perhaps you want me to go too badly. There may be something behind—"

"Stop right where you are, if you please, sir," broke in Tom Halstead, a decided trace of bitterness in his tone. "You're still more than half-inclined to suspect us boys of causing the loss of the papers you had hidden in the closet. I am not blaming you altogether, Mr. Seaton, though you are doing us a great injustice. But you *must* believe in us just at the present time, for going with us offers you your only chance of catching up with Dalton and saving your own friends of the syndicate. Come along, sir! Try to trust us, whether it seems wise or not, since it's your only chance."

The young skipper seized his charter-man by one arm, almost dragging him along. Yet Powell Seaton, who was in a state of horrible uncertainty, permitted this forcing.

Outside, on the porch, Captain Tom hesitated for a moment, then, after glancing at the guards, went on briskly:

"Mr. Seaton, I know you don't want to carry an armed force for purposes of attack on anyone, and you wouldn't have a right to do it, anyway. But, as we may be attacked, if we run afoul of Dalton and his friends, won't it be much better if you take at least a couple of your armed guards from this place?"

Nodding curtly, Mr. Seaton called to Hepton and Jasper, two of the guards, explaining that they were needed for a cruise on the "Restless." The pair followed along after the others.

"You can keep your rifles, just as well, in the motor room," suggested Captain Tom, and the fire-arms were placed below.

Hank had everything in readiness for casting off. Within forty-five seconds after boarding, the "Restless" was under way, poking her nose in a north-easterly direction.

"We'd better loaf later on, rather than now, Joe," proposed the young skipper. "See how much speed you can crowd out of the motors."

Powell Seaton chose to go aft, all alone, dropping into one of the deck arm-chairs. For a long time he remained there, moody and silent.

"What liner do you figure on Dalton trying to overtake and board?" queried Joe, coming up at last out of the motor room.

"Why, I don't just know," confessed Tom, pondering. "But I'll tell you what you can do, Joe. Leave Hank to watch the motors. You go to the wireless apparatus and send out the longest spark you can get. Direct your call to any vessel bound for Rio Janerio, or Brazil in general. If you get an answer from such a craft, ask her latitude and longitude, course and speed, so we can make for her directly."

As Joe nodded, then dropped down into the motor room, intending to go by the passageway under the bridge deck, Tom noted a lurking figure a few feet behind him.

"Hullo! What are you doing there, Jasper?" queried the young captain.

"Jest mindin' my own business," replied the man, with a half-surly grin.

"I'm minding mine, in asking you," retorted Halstead, quietly. "I don't like passengers so close to me when I'm handling the boat."

"I s'pose mebbe you don't," rejoined Jasper, yet making no move.

"Won't you take a hint?" asked Tom, rather bluntly.

"Where d'ye want me to stand?" asked the fellow, sulkily.

"You could go further aft, for instance," replied Tom. One hand on the wheel, he stood half-turned, eying this stubborn guard.

"Oh, all right," came gruffly from Jasper, as he started slowly aft.

"Maybe I'm wrong for thinking much about it," muttered Tom, under his breath, "yet it was this same man who was so close to us the other night when Mr. Seaton and I were talking about the papers hidden in the closet at the bungalow."

Two or three minutes later a slight sound caused the young skipper to turn with a start. He saw Jasper in the very act of fitting a wire-nipper to one of the parallel wires of the aerial of the wireless.

In an instant Captain Tom Halstead jammed his wheel and locked it. Then he dashed at the fellow.

CHAPTER XI
THE DRAB BOAT SHOWS HER NOSE

"You keep off!" snarled Jasper, drawing back on the defensive, holding the wire-nippers so as to use them in defending himself.

But, if the young captain of the "Restless" knew any fear, at such moments, he didn't permit others to see it. He neither stopped nor swerved. Ducking in under Jasper's extended right arm, Tom closed with the fellow, grappling.

"Confound ye! I'll have to throw ye over into the water!" growled Jasper, fighting for a hold around the boy's waist and behind his back. But Halstead fought to break the grip, at the same time yelling:

"Hank! Here, mighty quick!"

Jasper fought, trying to force the young commander to the rail. He had half succeeded when Hank Butts raced on deck. Hepton, the other guard, who had been lounging in the engine room, was right behind Butts. Both of them raced to reach the struggling pair. Hank caught Jasper at the waist-line, while Hepton took a hold at Jasper's neck, forcing the fellow back.

Then Tom sailed into the melee with renewed energy. Jasper was a powerfully-built fellow, but the three were too many for him. They tripped Jasper, throwing him to the deck, and Hepton sat upon his comrade's chest.

"Halstead! You others! What does this violence mean?"

Powell Seaton shouted the question sternly. He had been disturbed by the racket and now stood amidships.

"Get him over, face down," panted Tom. "We'll make sure of the fellow before we begin to explain. Hank, run for a pair of handcuffs!"

Butts was up and off like a shot, wholly liking the nature of his errand.

"Halstead!" raged Mr. Seaton. "I insist upon an answer."

"It's a case of sea-bullying—that's what it is," growled Jasper. "It's an outrage."

"Hepton," warned the charter-man, "get up off of Jasper's chest. Let him go."

"Don't you do it," countermanded Tom Halstead. "It won't be safe. This fellow is a snake in the grass. I caught him at his tricks."

Hepton had acted undecidedly for a moment. Now, he concluded to stand by the young captain.

In a trice Hank was back. Now the three assailed Jasper, rolling him over on his face. Tom Halstead, himself, fitted the handcuffs.

"Take the wheel, Hank, until I'm through with this," panted Tom, leaping up from the treacherous guard. The locked wheel was now steering the "Restless" over an erratic course, but Hank swiftly had the boat on her true course once more.

"I insist on knowing what this shameful business means," cried Mr. Seaton, glaring at his young skipper.

Tom Halstead Fitted the Handcuffs.

"I should think you might. It's an outrage!" shouted Jasper.

"This fellow," charged young Captain Halstead, "was in the very act of cutting the aerial wires with a wire-nipper when I caught him. Why, I can show you the nippers he had."

Tom wheeled, to make a quick search along the deck. Jasper grinned covertly for he had thrown the nippers overboard in the struggle.

"You see!" flared the prisoner. "He talks about nippers—but where are they?"

"Halstead," demanded Mr. Seaton, "do you intend to obey me by setting this man free until I've had an opportunity to investigate all sides of this remarkable charge?"

"No, sir, I do not," rejoined Halstead, quietly though firmly.

"Do you forget that I command here?" raged the charter-man.

"Pardon me, but you don't command," retorted Skipper Tom, respectfully. "It is true that you have this boat under charter, but I am the captain and one of the owners, and I must handle trouble aboard in the manner that seems best. I caught this man in a treacherous attempt to make our errand this afternoon quite useless. Jasper stays in irons until we reach port. I'm sorry to be so stubborn with you, Mr. Seaton, but, just now, you've a queer idea that I'm working against you. I must save you, sir, even from your own blindness. Hepton, will you help me take this fellow aft?"

"Surely," nodded the guard, who, while he had not seen the start of the trouble, much preferred believing Halstead to Jasper.

Seeing that resistance might bring him nothing but a beating, Jasper sulkily allowed himself to be led along the deck. Down into the cabin he was taken, there to be thrust into the starboard stateroom. Joe, from his wireless table at the forward end of the cabin, looked up with much curiosity.

"He was trying to snip the wires in your aerial," Halstead explained, after turning the key in the stateroom door.

"Glad you got him, then," nodded Dawson.

Mr. Seaton had followed as far as the doorway. There he halted, well convinced that he could not, at present, persuade the young skipper to change his mind.

"Now, if you'll be good enough to come up to the bridge deck, Mr. Seaton, I want to explain matters to you, sir," proposed the captain of the "Restless."

Rather stiffly the charter-man followed. Hepton, as though to show further good faith, took pains to remain aft.

"Do you remember the other night, when we were coming back with the guard for Lonely Island," began Tom, in a low voice, "that we found one of the new guards leaning well over the deck-house behind our backs?"

"I do," nodded Powell Seaton, coldly.

"That man, sir, was Jasper. To-day, when we are out trying to trace Anson Dalton over the open sea, I find that same fellow, Jasper, trying to cut the parallel wires of the aerial. Why should he do that unless he means to try to prevent our catching up with Dalton? Now, sir, putting two and two together, doesn't it seem mighty reasonable to suspect that Jasper overheard what we were saying the other night, and then watched his chance to steal the papers that you and I thought were so safely hidden in the cupboard at the bungalow? I know, Mr. Seaton, you feel that you have some reason for suspecting us boys. In view of what happened the other night, and again this afternoon, isn't it a whole lot more sensible to trace your misfortunes to Jasper?"

Powell Seaton, whose daze had continued ever since starting on this cruise, now pondered deeply, with knitted brows. At last, however, he looked up quickly, holding out his right hand, as he exclaimed:

"Halstead, I begin to believe that I have been too hasty and suspicious. I have hated myself for distrusting any of you boys, and yet—"

"And yet," smiled Tom, "you are beginning to feel that there is not as much reason for suspecting us as there is for believing that the guilt of a mean theft lies at someone else's door."

"I beg you to forgive me, Halstead, you and your mates. But I hardly know what I am thinking or saying. My mind is in too deep a turmoil."

"We'll forget it, Mr. Seaton," continued Halstead, as he pressed the other's hand. "*I* can, easily, and I hope you'll do your best to believe that you can trust us as fully as others have done."

"You may just as well come forward, Hepton," hailed Captain Tom, a few moments later. "And I want to thank you for the way you stood by me when I needed help so badly."

"Ever since we've been at the island I've felt that I didn't believe any too much in that man Jasper," muttered Hepton. "He has been acting queer some of the time."

"How?" asked Mr. Seaton.

"Well, for one thing, he always wanted the night guard duty. And he growled at taking the porch or the dock. What he wanted to do was to roam off about the island by himself. Whenever he came back he wanted to sit in your sitting-room, at the bungalow, and the fellow scowled if some of the rest of us showed any liking for staying in that sitting-room."

"What do you make of that, sir?" asked Captain Halstead, looking significantly at Powell Seaton.

"It sets me to thinking hard," replied that gentleman, gravely.

Hepton glanced with natural curiosity from one to the other. Then, finding that he was not to be enlightened as to what had happened ashore, he soon stepped aft again.

"Here's what you want to know, I reckon," announced Joe, in a low voice, as his head bobbed up out of the motor room. In one hand he held a slip of paper on which he had just taken down a message. "Twenty miles north of us is the Langley Line freighter, 'Fulton.' She's headed this way, and coming at fourteen knots."

Skipper Tom received the paper, studying the position and course as Joe had jotted them down.

"The Langley boats run to Rio Janeiro, don't they?" asked Halstead.

"Yes, and every boat of that line carries a wireless installation now, too," Joe continued. "She's the only boat that answered my hail."

"Take the new course, Hank," called the young skipper to the boy at the wheel, and rattled it off. The "Restless" swung around to a nearly northerly course.

"At her speed, and ours, it needn't be many minutes before we sight the 'Fulton,'" judged Halstead. "Hank, you keep the wheel. I want a chance to handle my glasses."

With the marine binoculars in his hand Skipper Tom soon began to sweep the horizon.

"There's what the wireless did for us," he chuckled to Mr. Seaton. "Without our electrical wave we wouldn't have known, for sure, that there was a Rio boat in these waters this afternoon. And, but for getting the 'Fulton's' position and course by wireless, we'd have swept by to the eastward, away out of sight of the freighter."

Within a few minutes more the young skipper, by the aid of his glasses, got a glimpse of a steamship's masts. A few minutes later the upper works of her high hull were visible.

"That's the 'Fulton.' I know the Langley type of freighter build," Halstead explained, eagerly. "We'll soon be close enough to see her name-plate through the glass. And—oh!—by Jove!"

Tom waved the glasses with a flourish, pointing, then handed them to Powell Seaton.

"Look right over there to the north-westward, sir, and you'll make out that drab-hulled seventy-footer. She's just coming into sight."

"I see her," nodded Mr. Seaton.

Captain Halstead took the glasses again, studying both the seventy-footer and the freighter intently, judging their relative speeds and positions.

"Dalton, or his friend, Lemly, has nicely calculated the drab boat's run," declared the young skipper of the "Restless," "Dalton's craft is in fine position to stop the freighter. But we'll reach the 'Fulton' first, and by some minutes, too, sir. The drab boat looks like a good one, but I believe we're a shade faster in the stretch."

"What are we going to do when we overhaul both craft?" wondered Powell Seaton, aloud.

"Why, sir, it will be easy enough to make the 'Fulton's' captain refuse to take any such passenger as Dalton."

"How?" demanded Mr. Seaton.

"Just inform the 'Fulton's' captain that Anson Dalton is a fugitive from justice. If you do that, the freighter's captain isn't going to take any chances on getting into subsequent trouble with Uncle Sam. The captain will simply decline to receive him as a passenger on the high seas."

Powell Seaton looked very cheerful for a moment. Then a look of dark doubt crossed his face.

"That will be all right, Halstead, unless it happens that the captain of the 'Fulton' is a man on the inside of some official affairs down in Brazil. If that be so, then your freighter's captain may recognize Dalton as a man of consequence—one to be served at all hazards. For, if a steamship captain of the

Langley line must be careful to stand well with the United States authorities, he must also be no less careful to keep in the good graces of some of the cliques of Brazilian officers. So what if Dalton goes aboard the freighter, and her captain sends us a derisive toot of his whistle?"

Tom Halstead's face showed his instant uneasiness.

"If that turns out to be the case, sir," he whispered, "you've lost your last chance to stop Anson Dalton. He goes to Brazil with all the papers for locating the diamond mine, and you and your syndicate friends lose the whole big game!"

CHAPTER XII
THE SEARCHLIGHT FINDS A "DOUBLE"

Yet, though his confidence in success had received a severe jolt, Captain Tom reached out for the megaphone.

"Run in straight and close, Hank," he ordered. "I want every possible second of conversation before that drab boat gets within talking distance of the 'Fulton.'"

The "Restless" and the freighter were now within a mile of each other, and almost head-on. The drab boat, about two miles away, had altered its course so as to pick up the freighter at a more southerly point.

"Run to your table, Joe," commanded the young skipper, "and notify the 'Fulton' that we are going to hail her for a brief pow-wow."

The speed with which young Dawson worked was shown by the fact that, when still half a mile away, the big freighter, hailed by wireless, began to slow down speed. It was plain that she was going to lie to in order to hear the whole of the hail from the "Restless."

"Great Scott, though! Look at that!" suddenly ejaculated Tom Halstead.

The drab seventy-footer had suddenly gone about, making fast westerly time for the shore.

"Go about after the seventy-footer, Hank," almost exploded Halstead, in the intensity of his excitement over this new move. "Dalton doesn't seem to want to try the freighter now. Follow Dalton back to shore."

"But the 'Fulton's' slowing down. You're going to show him the politeness of telling the freighter's captain what it was all about, ain't you?"

"Let Joe do it," replied Tom, tersely. "What's the wireless for?"

Just at this moment Joe Dawson appeared from below.

"Our apologies to the freighter, Joe," called Skipper Tom. "Tell him we're after the drab boat. Tell him that our game is to stop a fugitive from getting out of the United States."

Joe again appeared just as the freighter began to make full headway once more.

"Captain Carson sends you his compliments from the 'Fulton,' Tom, for chasing the fugitive off."

"And now, we're going to chase that fugitive in," uttered Halstead, grimly. "By George! Look at the way that drab boat is beginning to travel. Joe, we can't let her lose us in this fashion."

As the "Fulton" passed out hull down, and then finally vanished on the southern horizon, the chase after the drab seventy-footer became lively and exciting.

"Can you make out Dalton aboard of her?" asked Powell Seaton, as Tom stood forward, leaning against the edge of the forward deck-house, the marine glass as fast to his eyes as though glued there.

"No, sir. If Dalton is aboard, he's keeping out of sight in the cabin."

"Did you see, when the drab boat was more head-on, whether Lemly was at the wheel?"

"The man at the wheel wasn't Lemly, sir, though I believe that fellow is on board as the actual captain," Halstead answered.

"Humph! Is the Drab going to get away from us?" questioned Hank, wonderingly. "My, look at her bow cut water!"

"She's a faster boat than I thought," Tom responded. "But we don't mean to let her get away. Joe, how are we going on speed?"

"I couldn't get another revolution out of the twin shafts without overheating everything," Dawson replied, seriously. "Honestly, Tom, if this speed doesn't suit, I'm afraid we'll have to make the best of it."

"Then don't lose a single inch by bad steering, Hank," Halstead directed, looking around at his helmsman. "Whenever you want relief, let me know."

For five miles the drab seventy-footer kept her lead, though she did not seem able to increase it. That craft was still heading shoreward, and now the low, long, hazy line of the coast was in sight, becoming every minute more plain.

"They're going to head straight for the shore, unless they've some slicker trick hidden up their sleeves," declared Tom Halstead.

"I wonder that they're running so hard from us," mused Powell Seaton.

"Most likely, sir," responded the young skipper, "because Dalton and Lemly believe we have officers aboard. Of course they know—or suspect—that warrants are out charging them with stealing the 'Restless' the other night."

"Suppose Dalton and Lemly are not aboard that boat?" challenged Mr. Seaton, suddenly.

Tom Halstead's lower jaw sagged for just an instant.

"Of course, there's that chance. We may have been fooled, and we may be chasing a straw man in a paper boat right at this minute, sir. Yet, if Dalton were out on the water, with his stolen papers, he'd want to get nowhere else but to Brazil. If he isn't on the water, then he's not trying this route to your Brazilian enemies, and we might as well be out here as on Lonely Island."

As the boat in the lead neared the coast Halstead again kept the marine glass to his eyes.

"There's a little river over yonder," he observed.

"Yes; I know the stream. Hardly more than a creek," replied Mr. Seaton.

"Any deep water there, sir?"

"For only a very little way in. Then the stream moves over a pebbly bottom like a running brook."

"Then it looks, sir, as though Lemly—if he's aboard—plans to run in there and hustle ashore."

"Or else stay and fight," hinted Powell Seaton. "The place is lonely enough for a fight, if the rascals dare try it."

"Hepton!" summoned Halstead, a few moments later. "Don't you think you'd better get up your rifle? You don't need to show it, but someone may send us a shot or two from the drab boat."

Hepton sprang below, bringing up both rifles. Crouching behind the forward deck-house, he examined the magazines of both weapons.

"We're carrying load enough for a squad o' infantry," laughed Hepton, showing his strong, white teeth. "Let those fellers on the Drab try it, if they want to see what we've got."

The seventy-footer was shutting off speed now, going slowly into the mouth of the little river. Almost immediately afterwards her reverse was applied, after which she swung at anchor.

Tom, too, without a word to Hank, who stood by the wheel, reached over, slowing the "Restless" down to a gait of something like eight miles an hour.

"What's the order, sir?" he asked, turning to Mr. Seaton. "Are we to go in and anchor alongside?"

"I—I don't want to run you young men into any too dangerous places," began Powell Seaton, hesitatingly. "I—I—"

"Danger's one of the things we're paid for," clicked Tom Halstead, softly. "It'll all in the charter. Do you want to go in alongside?"

"I—I—"

Bang!

The shot came so unexpectedly that the motor boat boys jumped despite themselves. Hepton cocked one of the rifles, and was about to rise with it, when the young skipper of the "Restless" prodded the man gently with one foot.

"Don't show your guns, Hepton," murmured Tom. "Wait until we find out what that shot was meant for."

No one now appeared on board the drab seventy-footer. There had been no smoke, no whistle of a bullet by the heads of those on the bridge deck of the "Restless."

"That was intended only to make us nervous," grinned Captain Tom.

"Or else to show us that they have fire-arms," suggested Seaton.

"Well, sir, I'm headed to go in alongside, unless you give me other orders," hinted the young skipper.

"Cover about half the rest of the distance, then reverse and lie to," decided Powell Seaton. He now had the extra pair of marine glasses, and was attentively studying both the boat and the shore nearby.

Tom took the wheel himself, stopping where he had been directed. So neatly was headway corrected that the "Restless" barely drifted on the smooth water inshore.

There was now remaining less than an hour of daylight.

"I think I understand their plan, if Dalton is on board," whispered Mr. Seaton to his young captain. "Dalton is waiting until it is dark enough to slip ashore."

"Hm! There's one way you *could* stop that, if you want to take all the risk," ventured Halstead, grinning thoughtfully.

"How?"

"Well, if it's the plan of anyone aboard the drab boat to slip on shore under cover of darkness, then I could put our tender overboard and row Hepton to one bank of the river with his rifle. Returning, I could row you to the other shore, you to carry the other rifle."

"That would be a bold and open move," agreed Mr. Seaton, gasping at first, then looking thoughtful. "But look at that shore, Halstead. See the thick trees on either bank of the river. Hepton and I couldn't watch a lot of stretch on both banks."

"With our help from the boat you could, sir."

"Again, how?"

"Why, it's shallow enough to drop anchor right here, Mr. Seaton. Then, as soon as it grows the least bit dark, we boys could keep our searchlight turned on the drab boat so that you and Hepton could see every movement on her decks. From a quarter of a mile off you could see anyone swimming ashore and run to stop him. There's no difficulty about it, sir, except the risk."

"Hepton, I must talk that over with you," cried Powell Seaton. "I don't feel that I have any right to run you into too certain danger."

But Hepton smiled again in a way to show his white teeth.

"Don't worry 'bout me, Mr. Seaton. I feel big 'nough to take care of myself, and I enlisted for the whole game, anyway."

"You could keep watch right from this deck," Halstead added. "But then, if anyone slipped ashore from the Drab, you couldn't get on shore fast enough to follow through the woods. You'd lose the trail right after the start."

"Even if I were on shore, and Dalton walked right by me, what could I do?" pondered Powell Seaton. "Of course, I know the sheriff of the county would take him, for going aboard this boat and breaking it loose from the dock the other night. A United States marshal might arrest Dalton, on my request, for piracy in sailing away with the boat. But would I have a right to seize Dalton and hold him—even if able?"

"You can follow him until you *do* run Dalton into one of the law's officers," proposed Halstead.

"I believe I'm going ashore, anyway, to see what happens," announced Mr. Seaton, after giving the matter a little more thought.

"But let me go ashore, first, on the other bank," begged Hepton. "Then you can take second chance, sir."

"Very good, then," agreed the charter-man.

With the aid of his mates, Captain Tom had the anchor overboard, and the small tender alongside in a jiffy. Hepton stepped down into the smaller craft, carrying his rifle so that it could be seen. Tom himself took the oars to row.

"I'd better put you in on the bank to the left," whispered Halstead, and Hepton nodded.

They passed within forty yards of the stern of the drab boat, yet not a single human being appeared on that mysterious craft.

Having put Hepton on shore, Halstead rowed back for Mr. Seaton. Embarking this second passenger, Tom, this time, rowed a little closer to the seventy-footer lying at anchor in the river's mouth. Now, the head of a man unknown to either of them showed aft.

"Where you-all goin' with so many guns?" this man asked, in a half-jeering tone.

"Night hunting," retorted Tom, dryly, not feeling guilty of a lie since he was certain the other would not believe him.

Landing Mr. Seaton on the other river bank, the young captain of the "Restless" returned to his craft.

By now it was nearly dark.

"We may as well see how the searchlight is working," Joe Dawson suggested.

"Turn it on them, and sweep it around," responded Halstead.

The strong glare of light was found to be working satisfactorily. Dark came on quickly, still without any more signs of life aboard the Drab than had already been observed.

"Supper time, surely," announced Hank, in a glum voice.

"Don't bother about that to-night," objected the young skipper. "Slip down into the galley and make sandwiches enough for all hands. We can eat and watch—*must*, in fact, if we eat at all."

After the sandwiches had been made and disposed of the Motor Boat Club boys began to find the swinging of the light on the drab boat, on the water and on either river bank, to be growing rather monotonous.

"I wish something would happen," grumbled Hank.

"Now, don't start a fuss about that," yawned Joe. "Something is likely enough to start up at any second."

"It has started," whispered Tom Halstead, swinging the searchlight, just then, across the Drab's hull. "Look there!"

Two much-muffled figures, looking nearly identical, and each of the pair carrying a bag, appeared on deck amidships, one standing on each side of the deck-house. Then, as quickly, by their sides stood two other men who sprang to lower the two small boats that hung at davits. One muffled man and one helper embarked in each boat, the helper in each case rowing swiftly to either bank of the river.

"That's a queer game, but a clever one," muttered Captain Tom, swinging the glaring searchlight and watching.

"It'll mix up Mr. Seaton and Hepton all right," grimaced Joe Dawson. "Each will wonder whether *he* has Dalton on his side of the river, to follow."

Now, as quickly, the two boat-tenders rowed back to the Drab, and the boats were triced up in a twinkling.

"Say, they've got their anchor up!" cried Hank Butts, in a breathless undertone. "They're going to scoot out on us."

"Then I'm ready to bet," muttered Tom Halstead, "that neither of the muffled men that went ashore was Anson Dalton. They must be trying to throw our crowd off the trail, and now that seventy-footer is trying to get off with Dalton still aboard!"

Whatever the plan was, the Drab was now backing out of the river mouth and swinging around. So far none of her sailing lights were in evidence. She looked more like a pirate craft slinking out into the night on an errand of dire mischief.

Once out of the mouth of the river, the Drab swung around, then began to move ahead. By this time her prow was head-on for the "Restless," as though aimed to strike the latter craft amidships.

Then, as the Drab's speed increased, Tom Halstead vented excitedly:

"Jupiter! They're out to cut us in two while we ride here at anchor!"

CHAPTER XIII

TOM HALSTEAD—READY!

There was no time to raise the anchor. Even had this been possible, it would have been out of the question to get the motors started and running in time to get out of the Drab's way.

Captain Tom Halstead was taken wholly by surprise, yet he was not caught with his wits asleep.

"Make a dive for those sticks, fellows!" he shouted, bounding for the motor room hatchway. "If we get a chance we'll give 'em at least a pat for a blow!"

The sticks of firewood that they had used on the night of their long swim were in the motor room. Tom caught up his, wheeling to bound outside again. Joe Dawson was barely a step behind him.

But Hank—he went as though by instinct for the hitching weight that had already made him famous in the annals of the Motor Boat Club.

Swift as they were, the trio were back on deck just in time to witness the final manœuvre of the seventy-footer. That craft, not moving very fast, suddenly veered in its course.

Instead of cutting through the "Restless," the larger motor boat swung suddenly so as to come up alongside, rail to rail. And now the whole intention was manifest at a glance, for the figures of six men, with their caps pulled well down over their eyes, appeared at the Drab's rail.

"All hands to repel boarders!" sang out Captain Tom Halstead, his voice ringing defiantly. "Show 'em the best you can!"

Joe swung, with a single-stick trick he had learned and practiced. It was a feint, aimed at the first of the Drab's crew to try to leap aboard. The intended victim threw up his hands to ward off the blow from the top of his head, but he received, instead, a stinging, crushing slap across the face.

Tom thrust one end of his stick for the face of another of the boarding strangers. The fellow strove to protect his face, and would have guarded easily enough, but, instead, the other end of Tom's bludgeon struck him in the pit of his stomach, depriving him of all his wind.

"Woof!" grunted Hank, at the first sign of onslaught.

In both hands he clutched that business-like, though not formidable looking, hitching weight. One man set his foot on deck. Hank, almost with deliberation, dropped the weight on the toes of that foot.

There was a yell of pain. Snatching up the weight instantly, Hank let it fly forward and fall across the toes of another of the boarders.

Two of the strangers were limping now. Another was nursing an injured face, from Joe's heavy blow. Captain Tom's victim had fallen back aboard his home craft, gasping for breath.

The other two of the invaders got aboard the "Restless"—then wished they hadn't, for Hank pursued one of them with his terrifying hitching weight, while Tom and Joe divided the sole remaining enemy between them.

Hardly had the affair begun when it ended; it was all over in an instant. The two who had escaped injury leaped back aboard the Drab. Those who needed assistance were helped back. The Drab drifted away, her vagrant course unheeded at first, for it looked as though all aboard had taken part in that disastrous boarding enterprise.

Tom and Hank sprang for their own anchor, while Joe, as soon as he saw the big motor boats drift apart, dropped into the small boat of the "Restless" and rowed swiftly for shore. Hardly had he touched the beach when Powell Seaton, rifle in hand, bounded forth from cover.

"Put across, and see if we can get Hepton, too," directed the charter-man, in a low voice. "I stepped right up out of the bushes, almost into the face of the fellow who landed on my side of the river. It was neither Dalton nor Lemly. As soon as the fellow saw me he laughed, put a chew of tobacco in his mouth, and went on."

Hardly had Seaton finished speaking when Joe Dawson shot the bow of the little boat against the further bank. During this time Mr. Seaton had kept his eyes on the drab boat, holding his rifle in readiness in case another effort should be made to ram or board the "Restless."

"Oh, you-u-u-u!" called Joe, hailing. There was a sound in the woods, and then Hepton came into sight.

"Did you see the man who landed on your side?" whispered Powell Seaton, as Hepton reached the beach.

"Yes; he was just an ordinary roustabout chap," grunted Hepton, disgustedly. "I had no orders to follow *him*, so I didn't take the trouble."

"That's right. Jump in and we'll get aboard the 'Restless.'"

Hank had the motors working long before Joe returned with his two passengers, and was standing by. Captain Tom was at the wheel, but keeping the searchlight inquisitively on the Drab.

Now, the seventy-footer began to move off slowly down the coast, going at a speed of perhaps six miles an hour. Halstead, without waiting for orders, went in chase, keeping his place two hundred yards behind the other craft. All the while he kept the searchlight swinging over the Drab, from her port to starboard sides.

"That must annoy those fellows," observed Powell Seaton, with a chuckle, as he stood by the young skipper.

"I reckon it does," returned Tom, dryly. "But it also prevents their letting anyone off the boat without our seeing it. You see, sir, they're only about a quarter of a mile off the coast here. Their small boat could make a quick dash for the shore. Even a good swimmer could go overboard. I don't intend to let anyone get off that seventy-footer without our knowing all about it."

Halstead had not been silent long when he saw a bright flash from the Drab, aft. It was followed, almost immediately, by the sound of a gun. Then a bullet went by about two feet over their heads.

"That was meant for our searchlight," laughed Tom Halstead, coolly. "Those fellows want to put it out of business."

With an ugly cry Hepton leaned over the edge of the forward deck-house, sighting.

"Don't do that," called Captain Tom, sharply. Then he added: "I beg your pardon, Mr. Seaton, but I don't believe you want any shooting to come from us unless it's necessary."

"No, I don't," replied the charter-man, thoughtfully. "Dalton and Lemly seem willing to take desperate chances, acting like pirates, in fact. But we don't want to kill anyone, and, above all, we want to be very sure we have the law on our side."

"They fired our way," urged Hepton, rather stubbornly. "We have a right to defend ourselves."

"But they sent only one shot," replied Seaton. "They might afterwards claim that it was an accidental discharge. Unless they make it very plain that they're playing the part of pirates, we'd better take the best of care not to put ourselves wrong before the law."

"That's all right, sir," admitted Hepton. "But, while I'm willing to take any chances that go with my job, it doesn't seem just fair to ask me to be exposed to bullets from that other boat without the right to answer their fire."

"You can get down before the forward deck-house, Hepton," nodded Halstead, pleasantly. "You can't be hit through the deck-house."

"But you can be hit, fine," objected Hepton.

"Like Mr. Seaton," answered the young skipper, "I'd rather take the chance than do anything to put us in the wrong."

Grumbling a bit, though under his breath, Hepton seated himself where the forward deck-house would protect him. Joe remained leaning nonchalantly over the edge of the house.

"I wonder if they *will* dare to keep up a fusillade?" he presently said, watching the deck of the drab boat in the glare of light that Halstead now held steadily on it.

"If they fire another shot at us," replied Powell Seaton, "then Hepton and I will crouch over the forward deck-house, rifles ready, and fire at the flash of the third shot. We'll keep within the law, but we won't stand for any determined piracy that we have the power to resist."

"Take the wheel, Hank," called Tom, presently. Then the young skipper signed to his employer that he wanted to speak with him aft.

"Mr. Seaton," began Tom, "I want to ask you a few questions, with a view to making a suggestion that may be worth while."

"Go ahead, Halstead."

"You trust me now, fully? Have you gotten wholly over your suspicions of early this afternoon?"

"Halstead," replied the charter-man, in a tone uneasy with emotion, "I'm wholly ashamed of anything that I may have said or thought. You've shown me, since, how perfectly brave you are. I don't believe a young man with your cool, resolute grit, and your clear head, *could* be anything but absolutely honest."

"Thank you," acknowledged the young motor boat captain. "Now, Mr. Seaton, though the two sets of papers describing and locating your diamond field are out of your hands, don't you remember the contents of the papers well enough to sit down at a desk and duplicate them?"

"Yes; surely," nodded Mr. Seaton, slowly.

"You feel certain that you can seat yourself and write out a set of papers that would tell a man down in Brazil just how to locate the diamond field?"

"I can, Halstead. It would be a matter of some hours of writing, that's all. But why are you asking this? What plan have you in your mind?"

"Well, I've got a hunch, sir," replied Tom Halstead, quietly, "that you're never going to see the lost papers again. If Anson Dalton found you getting close to him, and knew you could seize the papers, he'd destroy them. It seems to me that our sole game must be to prevent his ever getting those papers to Brazil ahead of a second set that you can just as well write to-night."

"If we trail him all the time," replied Powell Seaton, thoughtfully, "we can know whether the fellow succeeds in getting away on a ship to Brazil. He can't go on that drab boat ahead, can he?"

"The seventy-footer would be quite good enough a boat to make the voyage to Brazil," Halstead answered. "So would the 'Restless,' for that matter. The only trouble would be that neither boat could carry anywhere near enough gasoline for such a voyage."

"Then Anson Dalton, if he gets away to Brazil, will have to board some regular liner or freighter? Well, as long as we keep him in sight, we'll know whether he's doing that."

"But Dalton will get desperate," Tom warned his employer. "While holding onto the papers he has succeeded in obtaining, he can make a copy, and he may very likely determine to send the copies to your old enemy, Terrero, by mail. Now, Mr. Seaton, it seems to me that your best hope is to duplicate the missing papers at once, and, if you can't find in haste a messenger you'll trust, then you had better send the papers by registered mail to your friends in Rio Janeiro."

Powell Seaton stared at the young skipper, going deathly pale.

"Captain Halstead, don't you understand that the possession of such a set of papers, at Rio Janeiro, would mean that the possessor could locate and file a patent to the diamond field, of which no one, save myself, at present knows the exact location? Why, even if the postal authorities do their very best to put the papers in the proper hands, anyone like a dishonest clerk might get the papers in his hands. The temptation would be powerful for anyone who had the papers to locate the mine at once for himself."

"I understand, fully," agreed Captain Tom. "But the whole thing has become a desperate case, now, and some desperate chances must be taken if you're to have a good chance to win out against Terrero and his crooked friends."

"Then you—you—honestly believe I'd better make out another set of papers and mail them to my friends of the syndicate, at Rio Janeiro?" faltered Mr. Seaton.

"Yes; unless you prefer to be almost certain of losing your fight for the great fortune. For Dalton, of course, knows that you can send a set of the papers by mail. He'll feel like taking the same desperate chance in order to have a better chance of getting in ahead of you."

"By mail—even registered mail?" groaned Mr. Seaton. "It seems an awful— desperate chance to take. Yet—"

"Prepare a duplicate set of the papers," proposed Tom Halstead, "and, if you'll trust me, I'll board the first Rio-bound steamer that we meet, and go through for you. I'll give you every guarantee that's possible to find your people in Rio and turn the papers over to them."

"Will you?" demanded Seaton, peering eagerly into his young skipper's eyes. "Then you'll trust me to go as your messenger to Rio?"

"Yes, in a minute, Halstead! Yet I'm thinking of the great danger you'd be running. At this moment Terrero's spies must be plentiful in Rio Janeiro. Why, even every steamer that leaves New York for Brazil may carry his men aboard, alert, watchful and deadly. You don't know what a man like Terrero is like. The constant danger to you—"

"Constant danger," laughed Tom Halstead, softly, "is something that most men learn readily to face. Otherwise, wars would be impossible."

"But that is very different," retorted Powell Seaton, quickly. "In war men have the constant elbow-touch, the presence and support of comrades. But you would be alone—one against hundreds, perhaps, at the very instant when you set foot ashore in Brazil."

"I'll take the chance, if you let me," declared Captain Tom. "But, now, sir, you're losing time. Why don't you go below, get writing materials, and start in earnest to get out the duplicate papers?"

"I will," nodded the charter-man. "Should I change my mind, it will be easy enough to burn the sheets after I have written them."

As Powell Seaton turned to go down into the cabin Joe Dawson called sharply: "Tom, something's up ahead! Come here, quickly!"

<hr>

CHAPTER XIV
GRIT GOES UP THE SIGNAL MAST

Even before Captain Tom turned he heard the sudden throb of the twin screws of the propellers, and felt the speed being reversed. That told him, instantly, that Joe had found some reason for stopping the "Restless" in a hurry.

As the young commander bounded forward the steady ray of his own searchlight showed him that the seventy-footer had also stopped her headway.

Hank was still at the wheel, but young Dawson was beside him on the bridge deck.

"There they go—dropping their anchor overboard," cried Joe, pointing. "The water's shallow along this coast, of course."

"We'll move right in, between that boat and the shore, and drop anchor, too," decided Captain Halstead, taking the wheel and reaching for the engine control. He sent the "Restless" slowly forward into place, then shut off headway, ordering:

"Joe, you and Hank get our anchor over. Dalton can't get anything or anybody ashore, now, without our knowing it."

"But what can his plan be, anchoring on an open coast?" demanded young Dawson, as he came back from heaving the anchor.

"Our job is just to wait and see," laughed Captain Halstead.

Mr. Seaton came on deck again, to learn what this sudden stopping of the boat meant.

"It's some trick, and all we can do is to watch it, sir," reported the young skipper of the "Restless," pointing to the anchored Drab. "Yet I think the whole situation, sir, points to the necessity for your taking my recent advice and acting on it without the loss of an hour."

"Either the registered mail, or yourself as a special messenger," whispered Seaton, hoarsely, in the boy's ear. "Yes, yes! I'll fly at the work."

"Don't hurry back below, though," advised Halstead. "Stroll along, as though you were going below for a nap. A night glass on the seventy-footer is undoubtedly watching all our movements."

As the two boats swung idly at anchor, on that smooth sea, their bows lay some three hundred yards apart. The night air was so still, and voices carried so far, that those on the deck of the "Restless" were obliged to speak very quietly.

Over on the seventy-footer but one human being showed himself to the watchers on the smaller boat. This solitary individual paced the drab boat's bridge deck, puffing at a short-stemmed pipe.

"I'd give a lot to be smart enough to guess what their game is," whispered Joe, curiously.

"It's a puzzle," sighed Captain Tom Halstead. "It looks, now, as though Dalton and Lemly are trying to hold us here while someone else does something on shore."

"Then you think the two who landed on either bank of the river—"

"We know that neither of them was Dalton or Lemly, but I'm beginning to suspect that one, or both, of those fellows carried messages, somewhere and of some nature. In that case, we're letting our curiosity hold us up here while the enemy are accomplishing something at some other point."

"Confound 'em!" growled Joe, prodding the bulwarks with his toe. "They're clever rascals!"

"Meanwhile," whispered Tom, "I've just been thinking of something else that we ought to be doing."

"What?"

"There may be another steamship for Rio Janeiro passing somewhere in these waters at any time. We ought to send out a call on the wireless at least once an hour. There's something else in the wind, old fellow, and we *do* want to know when the first steam vessel for Rio passes through these waters."

"Then I'll go below and get at work at the sending key," proposed Dawson. "Send out the wireless call once an hour, you say?"

"Yes; yet we don't want to forget that we're being watched all the time from that old drab pirate yonder. Don't let the enemy see you going to the cabin."

"I'll drop down into the motor room and use the passageway through."

Dawson was gone ten minutes. When he returned he shook his head, then stood looking out over the sea. Excepting the "Restless" and the drab seventy-footer there was no craft in sight. Not so much as a lighthouse shed its beams over the ocean at this point of the coast.

"Say, it's weird, isn't it?" muttered Joe Dawson. "We can't see a thing but ourselves, yet down in the cabin I've just been chatting with the Savannah boat, the New Orleans boat, two Boston fruit steamers, the southbound Havana liner and a British warship. Look out there. Where are they? Yet all are within reach of my electric wave!"

"There are no longer any pathless roads of the sea—not since the wireless came in," declared Tom Halstead. "If there were enough vessels to relay us we could talk direct with London now. The next thing will be a telephone in every stateroom, with a wireless central on the saloon deck or the spar deck. But gracious! We've been forgetting all about our poor prisoner in the starboard stateroom. He must have a royal case of hunger by now. Tell Hank to take him in some food and to feed the poor fellow, since he can't use his own hands."

Later time began to drag by. There were few signs of life aboard the seventy-footer. Sending Joe and Hepton down to the motor room berths as watch below, Tom kept Hank on deck with him. Bye-and-bye Joe and Hepton took their trick on deck, while Halstead and Hank Butts went below for some sleep. Through most of the night Powell Seaton remained hard at work over his writing, often pausing to read and make some corrections.

Morning found the two boats still at anchor. With sunrise came a stiffer wind that rocked the "Restless" a good deal.

"Now, look out for one of the sudden September gales," warned Captain Tom Halstead, as, after the second short sleep of the night, he came up on deck, yawning and stretching. He stepped over to read the barometer, then turned quickly to Joe.

"Looks like something's going to happen, doesn't it?" queried Dawson.

"Yes; there's a disturbance heading this way," admitted Tom, looking around at the sky. "Yet it may be hours, or a day, off yet. If we were going under canvas, though, I'd shorten it."

"The captain of the Drab evidently believes in being prepared," hinted Joe, nodding in the direction of the other craft. Two men were now visible on the deck of the seventy-footer. They were taking up anchor, though not doing it with either speed or stealth.

"I reckon we have to take our sailing orders from them," nodded the young skipper. "You'd better get the motors on the mote, Joe. I'll have Hank and Hepton help me up with our anchor."

Soon afterwards the Drab was heading north at a ten-mile gait; half a minute later the "Restless" started in leisurely pursuit.

After half an hour or so the Drab headed into another open roadstead, anchoring a quarter of a mile from shore. Tom dropped anchor some three hundred yards to the southward.

"Keep your eye seaward, Hank," directed the young skipper. "Joe, if you'll see whether Mr. Seaton wants anything, Hepton and I will keep a keen eye on the shore."

"Mr. Seaton is asleep in the port stateroom," Dawson reported back a moment later. "I've made eight calls through the night, but I'll get at the sending key again, and see whether there's anything in our line within hail."

Hardly had Joe Dawson vanished below when Skipper Tom uttered a sudden exclamation. A sharp, bright glint of light from under the trees on shore caught his watchful eye.

"Look there!" the young captain called, pointing to the flash.

"There's another," muttered Hank Butts, pointing further up the coast.

"By Jimminy, there's a third," cried Hepton, pointing.

"Signals for the Dalton-Lemly crew," uttered Tom, disgustedly. "*They* are getting news, now, and of a kind we can't read. Hank! Call Mr. Seaton. *He* ought to be on deck, watching this."

The charter-man was speedily up into the open.

In the meantime Joe, at the powerful sending apparatus below, sent the spark leaping across the spark-gap, and, dashing up the aerials, there shot into space the electric waves intended to be gathered in by any other wireless operator within fifty or sixty miles.

Crash-sh! Ass-ss-ssh! hissed the spark, bounding, leaping to its work like a thing of almost animal life.

Bang! This last note that came on the air was sharp, clear, though not loud. Whew-ew! A bullet uttered a swift sigh as it sped past the signaling mast twenty feet over the heads of the watchers of the "Restless."

"Confound it! Rascals on shore are shooting at us," exclaimed Powell Seaton, turning swiftly to peer at the forest-clad shore line.

"No; they're shooting at our aerials!" retorted Captain Tom Halstead.

Bang! Whe-ew-ew! Clash! Then there was a metallic clash, for the second rifle shot from the land had scored a fair bull's-eye among the clustered aerial wires. There was a rattle, and some of the severed wire ends hung down.

With an ugly grunt, Hepton bounded down into the motor room, passing up the two rifles.

"We must be careful, though," warned Mr. Seaton. "This time they're not shooting at us."

"Load and be ready, though!" uttered Captain Tom, dryly. "They soon will be shooting at us."

Several more shots clattered out, and two more of the bullets did further damage among the aerial wires. Then Joe came dancing up on deck, his eyes full of ire.

"The infernal scoundrels have put our spark out of business," he cried, disgustedly. "We haven't wire enough left to send five miles. Where do the shots come from?"

"From the shore," Halstead replied, "but see for yourself if you can locate the marksmen. We can't. They're using smokeless powder, and are hidden so far in under the trees that we can't even make out the flashes."

"It's out of my line to locate them," announced Joe Dawson, with vigor. "It's mine to see that the aerials are put on a working basis again."

He vanished, briefly, into the motor room, soon reappearing with a coil of wire and miscellaneous tools.

"Good!" commended Halstead, joyously. "Mr. Seaton, we have wire enough to repair a dozen smashes, if need be. On up with you, Joe. I'm at your heels."

Joe started to climb the mast, using the slightly projecting footholds placed there for that purpose. Tom let him get a clear lead, then started up after his chum.

From the shore broke out a rapid, intermittent volley. Steel-clad bullets sang a song full of menace about that signal mast.

"Come down, boys! You'll be killed!" roared Mr. Seaton, looking up apprehensively.

While Joe kept on climbing, in silence, Skipper Tom looked down with a cool grin.

"Killed?" he repeated. "Well, if we're not, we'll fix the aerials. We can't allow strangers to put us out of business!"

Joe found his place to go to work. Tom halted, with his head on a level with his chum's knees. From the shore there came another burst of rifle-fire, and the air about them was sternly melodious with the pest-laden hum of bullets. Two of the missiles glancingly struck wires just above Dawson's head.

In the lull that followed Joe's voice was heard:

"Hold the wire, Tom. Pass me the pliers."

CHAPTER XV

PLAYING SALT WATER BLIND MAN'S BUFF

"I've got to do something!" growled Hepton, his teeth tightly shut.

Raising his rifle to his shoulder, making his guess by sound, the man let two shots drive at the shore, not far back from the beach's edge. Then, after a pause and a long look, he let three more shots drive, slightly changing his sighting each time.

"Come on, Mr. Seaton," he urged. "They're firing on your skipper and engineer this time. It's up to us to answer 'em—clear case of self-preservation. The first *law* that was ever invented!"

Bang! bang! rang Seaton's rifle, twice. He, too, fired for the forest, near the beach. It was like the man to hope he had hit no one, but he was determined to stop if possible this direct attack on Tom Halstead and Joe Dawson.

Evidently the first sign of resistance was not to stop the bothering tactics of those on shore, for one wire that Joe was handling was zipped out of his hands.

"They mean business, the enemy," called down Skipper Tom, softly, to the tune of a low laugh. "But we'll get rigged, in spite of them. All we ask for is that they let us get the wire fixed often enough for a few minutes of sending and receiving once an hour."

Hepton and his employer continued to fire, using a good deal of ammunition. The guard was much more vengeful in his firing and in his attempts to locate the hidden marksmen than was Seaton.

"That's what those two men went ashore for last night," called down Halstead, quietly. "First of all, to fool us and get us guessing, and, next, to hunt up some of their own rascals for this work. The seventy-footer led us into this trap on purpose. Finely done, wasn't it?"

"It shows," retorted Mr. Seaton, wrathily, "that along this sparsely settled shore there is a numerous gang organized for some law-breaking purpose."

"Smuggling, most likely," guessed Tom. "And it must pay unusually well, too, for them to have such a big and so well-armed a crew."

Three more shots sounded from the shore. All of the trio of bullets went uncomfortably close to the young skipper and engineer, though doing no actual damage. Hepton, with his ear trained to catch the direction of the discharge sounds, changed his guess, firing in a new direction.

"There, it's done, until it's put out of business again," muttered Joe, finally. "Slide, Tom."

Almost immediately after Dawson disappeared the crash of the spark across the spark-gap and up the wires was heard. The young wireless operator of the "Restless" was making the most of any time that might be left to him.

"How about that storm that threatened last night, captain?" inquired Mr. Seaton. "Has it come any nearer?"

"There, It's Done," Muttered Joe. "Slide, Tom."

"No, sir," replied the motor boat captain, shaking his head. "It acted the way many September storms do on this coast. It passed by us, out to sea, and ought to be down by Havana by now. The barometer has been rising, and is at nearly the usual pressure. But I don't like the looks of the sky over there"—pointing.

"Why not?" queried the charter-man, following the gesture with his eyes.

"We'll be playing in great luck, sir," answered the young captain, "if a fog doesn't roll in where the storm threatened to come."

"Fog?" Mr. Seaton's tone had an aghast ring to it.

"Yes, sir."

"Are you sure, Captain?"

"No, sir. It's only a possibility, but a good one."

Hepton was making his rifle bark again, deep, snappy and angry in its throat, in answer to a challenge from shore, but Powell Seaton stood surveying the weather with a look of deepest concern.

Then he turned to regard the drab seventy-footer at anchor near by.

"It would be the enemy's real chance, wouldn't it?" he inquired.

"Just what I dread, sir," Captain Tom admitted. "Let us be wrapped in a thick bank of fog, and the Drab would be out of our vision and hearing in a very short time."

"Shades of hard luck!" groaned the charter-man, growing pallid.

Off on the seaward horizon an indefinite haze was soon observable. To the untrained eye it didn't look like much. Though Mr. Seaton spoke of it, he didn't appear much concerned.

"It'll be a pity to bother him until the time comes when he throbs with worry," thought Captain Tom Halstead, sympathetically. "But if that low-hanging haze doesn't spell t-r-o-u-b-l-e, then I've been raised among a different breed of sea fogs!"

The crashing of sparks over the spark-gap had ceased for the present, and Joe, reporting that there was no wireless craft within reach of his limited aerials, was on deck once more, waiting until the time should come around for another trial.

Hank had gone below to start the motors, connecting them with the dynamo, to renew the supply of electrical "juice" in the storage batteries, which was running low, as proved by the last message sent.

The chug-chug of the twin motors was heard over on the seventy-footer, and soon an unknown man, his cap pulled well down over his eyes, appeared at the stern of the Drab. He took a long, keen look at the "Restless."

"He's wondering if we're going to hoist the mud-hook," smiled Tom.

"And hoping that we are," grinned Joe. "Oh, but we must be an eyesore to those wistful scoundrels!"

Powell Seaton now spent most of his time gazing at the line of haze, which, by degrees, was growing bigger and coming nearer.

"Captain Halstead," he faltered, "I'm beginning to feel certain that you're a prophet."

"Or a Jonah?" laughed Tom, though it was not a very cheerful sort of laugh.

"No, no, no!" cried the charter-man, earnestly. "Never that! The little luck that I've had in these trying days has all come through you youngsters. Without you I'd have been flat on my back in the fearful game that I'm playing with such desperate hopefulness against hope. But I see our fog is coming in as a sure thing. If it envelops us, what can you do with regard to that drab-tinted sea-monster over yonder?"

"It depends upon the depth and duration of the fog, sir," Halstead answered. "We have our motors going. At the first strong sign of our getting hemmed in by it we'll lift our mud-hook [the anchor] and move in closer. If the fog isn't too thick we may be able to take up a position where we can at least observe her dimly. If she starts to pull out into a fog-bank, we'll follow at her heels, keeping as close as necessary to keep the Drab's stern flag-pole in sight. We won't lose her if there's any way of stopping it."

The advance guard of the fog was in upon them by the time that Joe went once more to his sending table in the forward end of the cabin. The light mist extended to the shore, though it did not altogether screen it. But the lookout on the Drab's deck appeared wholly watchful at the weather side of the craft.

"Not in touch with any other wireless boat yet," reported Dawson, coming on deck, presently.

"Look at that heavier white curtain rolling in," uttered Powell Seaton, in a tone near to anguish.

Whoever was in the drab boat's pilot house took occasion to toot derisively twice on the auto whistle.

"That's as much as warning us that their turn is coming," declared Mr. Seaton, wrathfully.

Their faces were wet, now, with the fog as it rolled in. Slowly the nearby shore faded, wrapped in the mist.

"We'd better get up anchor," decided Skipper Tom. "Come along, Hank, and you, Hepton."

As the anchor came up and was stowed, Captain Halstead moved the deck speed control ever so little. The "Restless" began to barely move through the water. They overhauled the seventy-footer, passing within a hundred feet of her starboard rail. Yet only the same deck watch appeared in sight. He favored those on the bridge deck of the "Restless" with a tantalizing grin.

Halstead slowly circled the drab seventy-footer, Mr. Seaton keeping ever a watchful eye on the stranger.

"There! They're hoisting anchor!" muttered the charter-man, at last.

"I saw 'em start," nodded the young skipper. "And the fog is growing thicker every minute."

"How are you going to beat them, if they try hard to get away?"

"I don't know," confessed Halstead, honestly. "We may keep 'em in trail, but the chances are all in favor of the drab boat."

Presently the seventy-footer slipped slowly away from her anchorage. Halstead promptly closed in, keeping not more than a hundred feet behind her drab stern. If the fog grew no heavier, and the enemy's speed no greater, he could maintain his position.

But the sea-born fog continued to come, looking as though it arrived in ever-increasing billows.

Once the seventy-footer's stern vanished for a moment or two. Tom, cautiously increasing the speed, soon came in sight of that drab stern once more.

"I don't want to croak, sir," warned the young motor boat skipper, "but, luck aside, it looks as though we're about done for in this salt water blindman's buff."

"I realize it," nodded Powell Seaton.

Just then the seventy-footer crawled ahead again into the fog, and was lost to the pursuer. Throwing the wheel somewhat to port, Captain Halstead tried to come up on the Drab's quarter. A full minute's anxious suspense followed, but the enemy's stern did not show through the white shroud of the atmosphere.

Then Halstead threw off the power without applying the reverse. The "Restless" drifted under what was left of her headway.

"They've done it," uttered Tom Halstead, grimly. "They've given us the slip—gotten away in this white mass of mystery!"

Shaking, Powell Seaton leaned against the deck-house, his face pallid with sheer misery.

CHAPTER XVI

A GLEAM OF HOPE THROUGH THE SHROUD OF FOG

Resting one hand lightly on the top spokes of the wheel, young Halstead turned to his employer with a look of keenest sympathy.

"Is there any order you wish to give now, Mr. Seaton?"

"What order can I give," demanded the charter-man, with a piteous smile, "unless it be to say, 'find the drab boat'?"

Tom made a grimace.

"Of course I know how senseless that order would be," pursued Seaton, with a nervous twitching of his lips. In fact, at this moment it filled one with pity, just to witness the too-plain signs of his inward torment and misery.

There was a pause, broken, after a few moments, by the charter-man saying, as he made a palpable effort to pull himself together:

"Halstead, you've shown so much sense all along that I leave it to you to do whatever you deem best."

Skipper Tom's brow cleared at once. A look of purpose flashed into his eyes.

"Then we'll keep eastward out to sea, sir, or a little bit to the northeast, until we get out in the usual path of the southbound steamers."

"And after that?" demanded Powell Seaton, eagerly.

"All we can do, sir, then, will be to wait until we get a wireless communication with other vessels."

"Go ahead, lad."

Tom moved the speed control slowly, until the "Restless" went loafing along at a speed of six miles an hour. Heading weatherward, he gave more heed to the wheel, for there were signs that the water was going to roughen somewhat.

"Hank!" called the young skipper, and Butts came to the bridge deck.

"Sound the fog-whistle every minute," directed Halstead.

"Too-whoo-oo-oo!" sounded the melancholy, penetrating note through the mist.

"Are you going to keep that up, Captain Halstead?" inquired Mr. Seaton, in instant apprehension.

"Got to, sir. It's the law of the ocean in a deep fog."

"But it signals our location to the enemy on the drab boat."

"If it keeps the seventy-footer within sound of our horn all the time," laughed Halstead, "so much the better. Then the Drab will be within range of our marine glasses when the fog lifts."

"It shows those rascals the direction of our course, too," cried Seaton, in a still troubled voice.

"We've got to observe the law, sir, even if *they* do break it," Tom gently urged. "That other boat's people have been acting like pirates all along, but that would be no excuse for us. What if we cut into a lumber-laden schooner, and sank her at once?"

Mr. Seaton was obliged to nod his assent.

"It's a fearfully tough piece of luck for us, this fog," Tom continued, feelingly, "but we've got to make the most of it."

"And, if Anson Dalton gets aboard any Brazil-bound steamer while we're in this fog, the whole great game for myself and my friends is lost," faltered Seaton.

"If that steamer has a wireless installation," retorted the young motor boat skipper, "then we've every chance in the world to reach her before the Drab possibly can. Joe will hear her wireless two hours or more before the other fellows can hear or locate a fog-horn."

"It's—it's a dreadful uncertainty that this fog puts upon us," groaned the unhappy charter-man. "Dalton may take advantage of this white shroud to run straight for the nearest post office and mail the papers that he stole."

Captain Tom's mildly warning look checked Mr. Seaton ere he had time to say more in the hearing of Hepton.

"If you'll come aft, sir, we'll talk this over," suggested Halstead, in a low voice.

"Gladly," murmured the charter-man.

"Now, then, sir," almost whispered the motor boat skipper, as he and his employer stood on the deck aft, "you've written out a duplicate of the papers that were stolen."

"I have the duplicate set in an inside pocket," responded Seaton, tapping his coat.

"Are you ready to chance the mailing of them?"

"It's—it's a fearful risk, a terrible one, even to think of sending such priceless papers by registered mail."

"At least, sir," urged Tom, "you would be sure the documents were properly started on their way."

"Yet with no surety that they wouldn't fall into wrong hands at the other end," shuddered Seaton.

"Then, since your life would undoubtedly be the forfeit if you attempted to take the papers yourself, will you trust me, or Joe, to board the first steamer we pick up by wireless?"

"Wh—what do you advise, Halstead?" queried Seaton, with the air and tone of a man tortured by uncertainty and hesitation.

"I advise, sir, your making a very definite move of one kind or another, without the loss of another hour," rejoined young Halstead, almost sharply. "Simply drifting in a fog won't settle anything."

"Oh, I know that only too well," replied Powell Seaton, desperately.

"Let us," proposed Skipper Tom, "take a northerly course. We'll try to pick up a Rio-bound steamship. Failing in that, let us put in for land, you to send the papers off by registered mail—or I'll take train for New York and go by the first boat."

"I—I'll do it," agreed Powell Seaton, falteringly. "Halstead, my boy, I've pondered and worried over this until my brain almost refuses to act. I'm glad to have your clearer brain to steady me—to guide me."

"Are your papers sealed?" asked Captain Tom, after a little further thought.

"No; but I can soon attend to that."

"I'd go below and do it, then, sir."

"Thank you; I will."

Powell Seaton, as he started down the after companionway, trembled so that compassionate Halstead aided him. Then, returning, the Motor Boat Club boy stepped steadily forward to the bridge deck.

Studying the time, Tom determined to keep to the present course for fifteen minutes more, and at the same speed, then to head about due north. This, he figured, would keep him about in the path of southmoving coast steamships.

Hank, who was still at the wheel, took the orders. Joe, after a glance at the bridge deck chronometer, dropped below on his way to his sending table. The crash of his call soon sounded at the spark-gap and quivered on its lightning way up the aerials.

"Nothing happening in my line," announced Dawson, soberly, when, some minutes later, he returned to deck.

Captain Tom stood by, almost idly attending to the fog-horn, though Butts would have been able to do that as well as steer.

"Did you get anything at all?" Halstead inquired.

"Nothing; not a click by way of answer," Joe Dawson responded. "I had half a hope that I might be able to pick up a ship that could relay back to another, and so on to New York. If that had happened, I was going to ask the companies direct, in New York, when their next boats would leave port. I'll do that, if I get a chance. I'm bound to know when to look for the next Rio boat."

"If this fog seems likely to last," resumed Halstead, "I've been thinking about increasing to ten miles and keeping right on toward New York."

"Bully!" enthused Dawson. "Fine!"

"Yes; so I thought at first, but I have changed my mind. If we get wholly out of these waters we might put a messenger aboard a steamship bound for Rio Janeiro, and then Dalton, by hanging about in these waters, might find a chance to board. If he suspected our messenger—and it may be you or I—it might be the same old Clodis incident all over again."

Joe's face lengthened.

"It's growing wearing, to hang about here all the time," he complained. "I'm near to having operator's cramp, as it is."

"Don't you dare!" Skipper Tom warned him.

"Well, then, I won't," agreed Dawson.

For four hours more the "Restless" continued nearly due north, at the same original speed of six miles an hour. Halstead began to think of putting back, slowly retracing his course. Joe went down for his regular hourly "sit" at the sending table.

"Hurrah!" yelled Dawson, emerging from the motor room several minutes later.

He was waving a paper and appeared highly excited.

"Picked up anything?" called Tom Halstead, eagerly.

"Yes, sirree!" uttered Joe, delightedly, thrusting a paper into his chum's hand. "The Jepson freight liner, 'Glide,' is making an extra trip out of schedule. Here's her position, course and gait. We ought to be up to her within two and a half hours."

Tom himself took the news to Powell Seaton. That gentleman, on hearing the word, leaped from the lower berth in the port stateroom.

"Glorious!" he cried, his eyes gleaming feverishly as he hustled into an overcoat.

Then he whispered, in a lower voice:

"Tom Halstead, you're—you're—It!"

"Eh?" demanded the young motor boat skipper.

"You'll take the papers on to Rio!"

A gleam lit up Halstead's eyes. Yet, in another instant he felt a sense of downright regret. He was not afraid of any dangers that the trip might involve, but he hated the thought of being weeks away from this staunch, trim little craft of which he was captain and half-owner.

"All right, sir," he replied, though without enthusiasm. "I'll undertake it—I'll go to Rio for you."

<hr />

CHAPTER XVII
WHEN THE MOTOR BOAT CLUB BOYS "WENT DAFFY"

All this had been spoken in whispers. Both Mr. Seaton and Tom Halstead were keenly aware of the presence of the prisoner in the starboard stateroom.

"You don't seem as overjoyed as I thought you might be," observed Powell Seaton, in a tone of disappointment.

"I'm going through for you, sir, and I'll deliver the papers into the proper hands, if I live," replied Tom Halstead.

"And you're not afraid of the big chances of danger that you may be running?" persisted his employer.

"Why, I believe every human being has times when he's afraid," Skipper Tom replied, honestly. "But I shan't be any more afraid than you've seen me once or twice since this cruise began."

"Then I'll bet on your success," rejoined Mr. Seaton, holding out his hand, which the young motor boat captain grasped.

"Suppose we go on deck where we can talk a little more safely, sir," whispered Tom.

They made their way above and forward.

"Any further word, Dawson?" inquired the charter-man.

"I haven't signaled since I brought up that last message," Joe replied.

"Oh, of course not," retorted Powell Seaton. "It was an idiotic question for me to ask, but I'm so excited, boys, that I don't pretend to know altogether what I'm talking about."

Captain Halstead bent forward to look at the compass. He found Hank Butts steering as straight as the needle itself pointed.

"What on earth can I do to pass the time of waiting?" wondered Mr. Seaton, feverishly.

"Eat," laughed Tom. "You haven't had a meal since I don't know when. Give me the wheel, Hank, and see what you can fix up for Mr. Seaton in the way of food."

Yet, poking along at that slow rate of speed, cutting through the fog but not able to see a boat's length ahead, proved an ordeal that tested the patience of all.

After awhile Joe returned to the sending table, in order to get in touch with the "Glide" and make sure that the two vessels were still approaching each other head-on.

"It's wonderful—wonderful, this wireless telegraph that keeps all the great ships and many of the small ones in constant communication," declared Powell Seaton, coming up on deck after having finished his meal. "Yet it seems odd, doesn't it, to think of even freight boats carrying a wireless installation?"

"Not when you stop to consider the value of the freight steamships, and the value of their cargoes," rejoined Tom Halstead. "If a ship at sea gets into any trouble, where in older times she would have been lost, now all she has to do is to signal to other vessels within two or three hundred miles, and relief is sent on its way to the ship that needs it. In the case of a freight steamer the wireless aboard means greater safety for the crew and often saves the owners the cost of ship and cargo. The Standard Oil people were among the first to think of the wireless for cargo-carrying boats. They installed the wireless on their tank steamers, and it wasn't long before the owners of other freight vessels realized the value of such an installation. Now, every freight boat that amounts to much has the wireless aboard."

"You speak of the wireless being used at a distance of two or three hundred miles," pursued the charter-man. "Dawson can't send the electric wave that far, can he?"

"No, sir; because our signal mast is shorter than that on a big steamship. The length of our aerials is less. Still, we can handle a message for a pretty good distance."

"What distance, Halstead?"

"Why, our ideal distance is about sixty miles; we can make it seventy easily, and, under the best conditions, we can drive a message, so that it can be understood, for about ninety miles. But that doesn't really hold us down to even ninety miles. If there's a wireless ship within our radius we can ask her to relay for us. With a few ships spread out at proper intervals we could easily wire direct from the 'Restless' to the coast of England."

"Joe," called Tom to his chum as the latter came on deck between wireless performances, "do you notice that the fog is lightening off to weatherward?"

"Yes; the fog is heaviest off to westward, and we've been working out of that."

"By the time we reach the 'Glide' I believe we're going to have some open weather around us."

"It will be fine if we do," nodded young Dawson. "It's nasty work going up alongside of a big ship when you can't see fifty feet away."

As they watched and waited, while the "Restless" stole slowly along, the fog about them became steadily lighter, though off to the westward it remained a thick, dense bank.

"Say, it'd be great to have four or five miles of clear sea around us, so that we could see whether the seventy-foot boat has kept to anything like our course," declared Hank.

At last the "Restless" came to within twenty minutes' hailing distance of the "Glide," as the young motor boat skipper figured it. Then, a few minutes later, a deep-toned fog-horn came to them faintly. As the minutes passed, now, this blast became heavier and nearer.

"I've only a few minutes left with you, Joe, old chum," declared Captain Tom, with a half-sigh. "You'll take great, good care of the dear old craft, I know, while I'm gone."

"As soon as Mr. Seaton is done with the boat I'll tie her up until you get back—that's what I'll do," grunted Dawson. "No sailing without a skipper for me."

"You needn't look so bad about it, Cap," grinned Hepton. "I wish it was me, cut out for a long trip to Rio and back. Maybe I wouldn't jump at such a chance. Some folks are born lucky!"

Too-woo-oo!

The oncoming steamship's deep fog-horn sounded loud and sullen, now. Tom Halstead, still at the wheel, was peering constantly forward for the first glimpse of the freighter, for the fog had lightened much by this time.

"There she is!" hailed keen-eyed Joe, on the lookout for this sight. "You can just make out her bow poking up through the fog. She must be a thousand feet off yet."

With two boats approaching each other, this distance was, of course, quickly covered. Finding that he could see the other craft at such a distance, Skipper Tom threw on a little more speed, making a wide turn and so coming up alongside on a parallel course.

"Take the wheel, Hank," directed the young skipper, seizing the megaphone and stepping to the port rail.

"'Glide,' ahoy!" bawled Halstead through the megaphone.

"'Restless,' ahoy!" came back from the freighter's bridge.

"Lie to and let us come alongside, won't you? We want to put a passenger aboard."

"Passenger? Where for?"

"Rio, of course. That's where you're bound, isn't it?"

"You'll have to be mighty quick about it," came the emphatic answer. "We can't afford stops on our way."

"We may want to delay you a few minutes," began Tom.

"Few minutes, nothing!" came the gruff retort. "We can't be held up in that fashion."

"We can pay for all the trouble we put you to," retorted Halstead. Powell Seaton produced and waved a bulky wad of banknotes.

"Oh, if you want to pay extra, above the fare, it'll be a little different," came, in mollified tones, from the bridge. The captain of the "Glide" was now much more accommodating. The fare received from a passenger put aboard in mid-sea would go to the owners of the freighter. But any extra money, paid for "trouble," would be so much in the pocket of the "Glide's" sailing-master.

Several new faces appeared at the rail of the freighter, as that big craft slowed down and one of her mates superintended the work of lowering the side gangway.

"Hullo, lobster-smack!" roared one derisive voice above the freighter's rail.

"Say," called another voice, jeeringly, "it may be all right to go lobster-fishing, but it's no sort of good business to leave one of your catch of lobsters in command of even a smack like that!"

Tom Halstead reddened angrily. One of his fists clenched unconsciously as he shot a wrathful look upward at the rail.

"Say, you mentally-dented pilot of a fourth-rate peanut roaster of a boat, do you go by craft you know without ever giving a hail?" demanded a mocking voice, that of the first derisive speaker.

Standing at the rail of the "Restless," Tom Halstead almost dropped the megaphone overboard from the sheer stagger of joy that caught him.

"Hey, you Ab! You worthless Ab Perkins!" roared the young motor boat skipper, in huge delight. "And you, Dick Davis!"

The two who stood at the "Glide's" rail overhead, and who had called down so mockingly, stood in uniform caps and coats identical with those worn by Halstead and his mates aboard the motor boat. They wore them with right, too, for Perkins and Davis were two of the most famous of the many youngsters who now composed the Motor Boat Club of the Kennebec.

"Hey! What's this?" roared the usually quiet Joe Dawson, his face wreathed in smiles. He almost danced a jig.

Hank Butts had never before seen either Davis or Perkins, but he knew about them, all right. He knew that uniform, too, the same that he wore.

"Now, then—altogether!" yelled Hank. "Give it with a roar, boys!"

Powell Seaton stared in bewildered amazement. So did officers, crew and others at the "Glide's" rail and on her bridge.

For five lusty young Americans, all wearing the same uniform, all bronzed deeply with the tan that comes of the gale and the sun, all keen-eyed, quick and sure as tars ever are, roared in mighty chorus:

"M-B-C-K! M-B-C-K! Motor Boat Club! WOW!"

CHAPTER XVIII
THE FIRST KINK OF THE PROBLEM SOLVED

Again the roaring chorus rang out.

"What's this? College boys' joke on me, or a floating mad-house?" huskily roared down the freighter's captain from the bridge.

"It's all right, captain," sang back Tom Halstead. "We'll make it plain to you as soon as we get a chance. We're neither as bad nor as dangerous as we seem."

The "Glide's" headway had all but ceased by this time, and the side gangway was at last in place. The "Restless" was run in close, while Hank stood up on the top of the forward deck-house with a coil of line, waiting until it came time to leap across onto the platform of the freighter's gangway and make the line fast.

As quickly as the line was secured Captain Tom Halstead followed Butts, and dashed on past him up the steps of the gangway. Ab and Dick came down to meet him, each grabbing one of the young skipper's hands and wringing it.

Then they turned to give the same greeting to Joe Dawson, who gasped:

"Gracious, but it *does* seem good to meet fellows of the Club and from the old home town at that!"

Mr. Seaton, though following in more leisurely fashion, now passed them, going on up to the deck. There he met Captain Rawley.

"Don't mind what my young men do, captain," begged the charter-man, "and don't mind if they delay you for a few minutes. I'll make good the damage."

"Help yourself to a little of my time, then, sir," grimaced the freighter's captain. "Anything that I can spare from the proper time of the run, you understand."

"How on earth do you fellows happen to be on this ship, of all places in the world?" demanded Tom Halstead.

"Easy enough to explain," laughed Dick Davis. "Port authorities at Rio were good enough to order six motor boats for harbor purposes. My dad got the chance of building the boats at his yard at Bath. The Rio motor boats are on board, down in the hold, and Ab and I are sent along to deliver the motor boats, put them in running order at Rio, and, if necessary, teach the natives how to run such craft."

"Did you fellows know we were signaling you by wireless?" Joe was asking Ab Perkins. "Did you know that you were going to see us?"

"Didn't know a blessed thing about it," admitted Ab Perkins, almost sheepishly. "Dick and I were asleep in our stateroom. We were getting ready to come out on deck when we felt the old tub slackening speed. Then we came out to see what was happening. We looked over the rail, and—*wow!*"

Ab again seized Joe Dawson's hand, giving it another mighty shake. Then the irrepressible Ab reached out for Tom's hand, but Dick Davis was drawing Halstead up on deck.

Readers of the first volume of this series will remember both Ab and Dick well. They, too, were boys born near the Kennebec River, and took part in the stirring adventures narrated in THE MOTOR BOAT CLUB OF THE KENNEBEC, just before Tom and Joe left for the next scenes of their activities, as related in THE MOTOR BOAT CLUB AT NANTUCKET and THE MOTOR BOAT CLUB OFF LONG ISLAND. Ab Perkins and Dick Davis were two of the most valued of the early members of the Club.

All in a twinkling, Tom Halstead was seized by an idea. He looked about for Powell Seaton, saw that gentleman talking with Captain Rawley, and caught the charter-man's eye.

"See here, Mr. Seaton," whispered Halstead, as soon as he had gotten his employer aside, "there's no great need for me to go to Rio."

"No?"

"Of course not. Give the papers to Dick Davis, with exact instructions as to who is to receive them at Rio Janeiro, and those papers will get into exactly the hands for which you intend them."

"You feel certain of that, Halstead?" demanded Powell Seaton, his voice tremulous with anxiety.

"Absolutely sure, sir. Dick Davis can be trusted as long the world holds together. There isn't the faintest yellow streak in him, either. Square, straight, keen, brave—that's Dick Davis. And Ab Perkins would go through the jaws of anything with Davis! Why, Mr. Seaton, they're Motor Boat Club boys! You can trust them to the same degree as you're willing to trust me. Moreover, they're going down to Rio on a mission to the Government. They've got a better chance to get ashore, unmolested and unwatched, than any other stranger would have."

"Get your friends together, then, somewhere where we can have a private corner," begged Powell Seaton. "We'll talk this matter over—we've got to talk like lightning, at that."

While Mr. Seaton sought Captain Rawley, Tom shot back along the deck to where Joe, Hank and the two Rio-bound members of the Motor Boat Club stood talking.

"Hank," said Tom, in a low voice, "Hepton is all alone down on the 'Restless,' except for our prisoner aft. Hepton may be all right, and I think he is—but one of our own crowd ought to be on board our boat."

"I'll be the one, then," half-sighed Hank Butts, turning to descend the side gangway.

Captain Rawley promptly agreed to turn his own cabin over to the friends who wanted a private chat.

"But only for five minutes, mind you," he insisted. "Then I must be on my way."

Behind the closed door of the captain's room Powell Seaton and Tom Halstead swiftly explained what was wanted.

"Will we do it?" said Dick Davis, repeating the question that had been asked him. "Why, of course we will. There's only one answer possible. Tom Halstead is fleet captain of the Motor Boat Club, and a request from Captain Tom is the same thing as an order."

"You will go straight to the American consulate at Rio Janeiro, then," directed Mr. Seaton. "From the consulate you will send a messenger to bring to you Shipley D. Jarvis, whose address is the American Club. The American consul will be able to assure you that it is Shipley D. Jarvis who comes to you. You will turn over these papers to Mr. Jarvis in the presence of the American consul. A letter from me is in the envelope with the papers. That is all, except—"

After a brief pause Mr. Seaton went on to caution Dick Davis and Ab Perkins as to the dangers against which they must guard on the way. This Tom Halstead supplemented with an exact description of Anson Dalton and of Captain Dave Lemly, of the now seized "Black Betty."

"Either, or both, of the rascals may board this ship a little further along," cautioned Mr. Seaton. "Night and day you must be on your guard against them."

Then Tom Halstead quickly outlined to Davis a system of apparently common-place wireless messages by means of which Davis might be able to keep Mr. Seaton informed of the state of affairs, for some days to come, on board the "Glide."

Some further last instructions were added. Powell Seaton wound up by forcing a few banknotes into the hands of both these unexpected messengers.

"Wait until we've succeeded," proposed Dick Davis.

"This is for expense money, for sending wireless messages, and other things," replied Mr. Seaton. "Your real reward will come later on."

"When we've succeeded," nodded Davis.

So much time had been taken up by this talk that now all had to step out on deck.

"We're ready to go aboard our boat, sir," Skipper Tom reported.

"You and Dawson go, Halstead," nodded Mr. Seaton. "I want not more than sixty seconds with Captain Rawley in his own room."

When the charter-man of the "Restless" came out once more the thick pile of banknotes in his pocket had grown a good deal thinner, but Captain Rawley had been enlisted as a friend to the cause.

"Good-bye, old chums," cried Dick Davis, gripping a hand of Tom and Joe with each of his own.

"Good-bye! Good luck now, and all the way through life!" murmured Tom, earnestly, and with a hidden meaning that Davis caught.

As speedily as Tom and Joe had assisted Powell Seaton aboard the motor boat, Hank cast off, while the crew of the "Glide" began to raise the side gangway.

There were more rousing farewells between the two groups of Motor Boat Club boys. Then the hoarse whistle of the "Glide" sounded, and the freighter began to go ahead at half-speed.

The "Restless" fell away and astern, yet she followed the freighter. That she should do so had been understood with Captain Rawley, and with Dick and Ab. Powell Seaton intended to keep the "Glide" within sight for at least thirty-six hours, if possible, in order to make sure that the seventy-foot drab boat did not attempt to put Anson Dalton or any other messenger on board.

"If we stick to the sea for a hundred years, Joe," laughed Skipper Tom, as he followed the bigger craft at a distance of eight hundred feet, "nothing as lucky as this is likely to happen again. I was afraid I was booked for Rio, for sure, and it made me heartsick to think of leaving the 'Restless' so long and living aboard a big tub of an ordinary, steam-propelled ship!"

"I've taken the step, now, and can't very well change it," declared Mr. Seaton, who looked both pale and thoughtful. "Halstead, all I can hope and pray for is that your comrades on the ship ahead are as clever and watchful, as brave and honest as you think."

"If wondering about Dick and Ab is all that ever worries me," laughed Tom Halstead, easily, "I don't believe I shall ever have any wrinkles. I know those boys, Mr. Seaton. We were born and raised in the same little Maine seacoast town, and I'd trust that pair with the errand if it were my own diamond field at stake."

The fog had lifted sufficiently, by this time, so that clear vision was to be had for at least a quarter of a mile.

Skipper Tom whistled as he handled the wheel. Joe Dawson was so relieved in mind that, after a careful look at the motors, he threw himself upon one of the berths opposite and dozed. Hank put in his time looking after preparations for supper.

"What ails you, Halstead?" demanded Seaton, pausing abruptly beside the young skipper.

For the boy had turned, suddenly, to a sickly pallor.

"It has just struck me, sir," confessed the young motor boat skipper, "that, if Dalton has the slightest suspicion of what we've done to outwit him, he's just the man who will be desperate enough to put his whole set of papers in at the nearest cable office for direct sending to Rio Janeiro!"

CHAPTER XIX

HELPLESS IN THE NORTHEASTER!

"I've already thought of that," nodded Powell Seaton.

"And it doesn't worry you, sir—doesn't make you anxious?" questioned Captain Tom Halstead.

"No. Of course, Dalton might cable the full contents of the papers. If the paper could fall only into Governor Terrero's hands it would be well worth the cable tolls. But if such a cablegram were sent, openly, to Terrero, or one of his representatives, it would have to go, first of all, through the hands of the Government officials who have charge of the cable."

"But couldn't Terrero fix that?" asked Halstead.

"No; Rio is out of his state, and beyond the sphere of his strongest influence. Now, if I were to land in Rio Janeiro, I would be arrested on a warrant issued by Terrero's judges, up in the state of Vahia, and I would have to go to Vahia for trial. Undoubtedly Terrero's rascally officers would shoot me on the way, and report that I had tried to escape."

"Then what harm could it do to Terrero's chances for Dalton to send him the cablegram direct?"

"Why, either the cable officials in Rio are very great rascals, or else they are honest officials. If they are rascals, they might hold the cablegram long enough to act for themselves on the information it contained. On the other hand, if they are honest officials, then they would undoubtedly notify the Government of such a stupendous piece of news. The Government would then very likely take charge of my diamond field itself, which would be wholly legal, for the Government already owns many, if not the greater number, of the producing diamond fields of that country. So, if the Government, acting on information from its cable officials, took possession of the news and of the diamond field, what good would the cablegram do Governor Terrero? No; you may be very sure that Dalton won't send the contents of the papers by cablegram. He undoubtedly has the strongest orders from Terrero against doing that."

"I feel better, then," Tom admitted. "For the moment it came over me, like a thunderbolt, that Dalton might nip all our work in the bud by sending a cablegram. Still, couldn't he send it by code?"

"No; for only the ordinary codes can go through the Brazilian cable offices, and the Government officers have the keys to all the codes that are allowed. Rest easy, Halstead; Dalton won't attempt to use the cable."

"Then, if he doesn't get aboard the 'Glide,' we'll beat him out to Brazil— that's the surest thing in the world!" cried Tom, with as much enthusiasm as though the great fortune at stake were his own.

They were still following in the wake of the "Glide." Once in a while Dick Davis or Ab Perkins had the operator on the freighter flash back a wireless message of a friendly, personal nature. Joe answered all these.

For thirty-six hours this pleasant stern-chase lasted. By night the helmsman of the "Restless" kept the searchlight enough in use to make sure that the drab boat did not appear.

"Dalton and Lemly lost the 'Glide,' if they were looking for her, in the fog," chuckled Halstead, in huge satisfaction. "Any Rio-bound boat they can catch now is hopelessly to the rear of the 'Glide,' I reckon."

Joe, by wiring back, and asking other wireless vessels to relay, from time to time, had ascertained that there was no other steam vessel, bound for Rio, in close pursuit.

Mr. Seaton took his trick at the wheel occasionally. So did Hepton. Joe gave most of his time to the wireless installation, though he maintained charge of the motors, Hank doing most of the work there. All had sleep enough during the cruise south. Joe used some of his spare time in carrying out his former plan of connecting the wireless table with the helmsman by means of a speaking tube.

They were well down the coast of Florida when even anxious Powell Seaton declared that there was no need of cruising longer in the wake of the "Glide." He felt certain that the freighter had entirely eluded the vigilance of those on board the drab boat.

By this time the supply of gasoline was nearly out. Tom had cautioned the charter-man that so long a run would use up about the last of their oil. There was, however, a small sail fitted to the signal mast. Now, when the crew of the "Restless" turned back, the sail was hoisted and power shut off.

"We've oil enough to run perhaps three-quarters of an hour, sir," the young skipper explained. "We'll have to use that up in making port when we get in sight."

Sailing aboard the "Restless" proved lazy work at the outset. With this small sail there was not wind enough to carry the boat at much more than two miles per hour on her northwest course for the nearest Florida town where gasoline was likely to be had.

"We'll have a jolly long sail of it," laughed Skipper Tom, "unless the wind should freshen."

"Well, we don't care," smiled Mr. Seaton. "At least, you won't be overworked. And our minds are easier—mine especially."

"All of us have easier minds," Halstead retorted. "Don't you understand, sir, that the rest of us have taken this whole business to heart? We couldn't be more concerned than we are to see the affairs of our charter parties come through all right."

"Oh, I believe that," nodded Powell Seaton. "You boys have been the strongest sort of personal friends to me in my troubles. You couldn't possibly have made my affairs, and my dangers, more thoroughly your own troubles."

Two hours later a wireless message came back from the "Glide." It was from Dick Davis, and couched in vague terms, but meant to inform those aboard the "Restless" that the drab seventy-footer was still out of sight. An hour after that a second message reached the motor boat. Soon after the "Restless" found herself unable to answer, though still able to receive.

"Hank, are you feeling particularly strong to-day?" inquired Mr. Seaton.

"I'm always strong, sir," replied the young steward.

"Then why not rack your pantry stores in order to supply the biggest thing in a meal for all hands this evening? I feel more like eating than I have any day in a month."

"You'd have to go to a sure-enough number-one hotel to find a better meal than I'll put up for this evening," retorted Hank, grinning gleefully, as he started for the galley.

In such lazy weather Tom Halstead felt that he could go below for a nap, especially as Joe was around. Hepton was left at the wheel. Tom speedily closed his eyes in one of the soundest naps he had enjoyed in many a day. He was awakened by Hank, who came into the stateroom and shook him by the shoulder.

"Weather's all right, up to now," Butts informed the young captain. "Still, we don't like the looks of the sky, and the barometer is beginning to show signs of being eccentric. Won't you come up on deck for a minute, anyway?"

Tom was out of his berth in a twinkling. There was enough of the sea-captain in him for that. The instant he reached the deck his gaze swept around anxiously, inquiringly, at the sky.

"The clouds up on the northeast horizon don't look exactly friendly, do they?" he inquired of Joe.

"Don't know," replied Dawson. "Haven't seen enough of them yet."

"I'm thinking you will, soon," replied Halstead. "How's the wind been?"

"From the east, sir," replied Hepton, who was at the wheel.

"It's working around to northeast, now," muttered Halstead. "And it was almost from the south when I turned in."

Tom stood by the barometer, watching it.

"Trouble coming," he said, briefly.

81

Within half an hour his prediction began to be verified. The darkish, "muddy" clouds first seen on the northeast horizon were looming up rapidly, the wind now driving steadily from that quarter. Even with all the smallness of her single sail the "Restless" was heeling over considerably to port.

"Lay along here, Hank, and help me to put a double reef in the sail," Tom ordered. "I don't want this little bit of canvas blown away from us."

As Tom called, he eased off the sheet, and Hepton lounged away from the wheel.

"Too bad," muttered Hank Butts. "We've been making a good four knots since the wind freshened."

"I'm out of a guess if there isn't a wind coming that'd take a sail out of its fastenings in ten seconds," rejoined Halstead, working industriously with the reeves.

A light squall struck them before the boys had finished their task.

"A September northeaster along this coast is no laughing matter, from all I've heard of it," Tom explained as the two boys took the last hitches. "Now, come on, Hank. We'll hoist her."

With long rhythmic pulls at the halyards Tom and Butts got the shortened sail up, making all secure.

"You'd better take the wheel, Joe," sang out the young skipper. "Hepton, stand by to give a hand if the helm moves hard."

"You seem rather excited over a pleasant breeze like this," observed Powell Seaton.

"Wait," said Tom, quietly. "I only hope I am taking too much precaution. I've never handled a boat along the Florida coast before, you know, sir, so it's best to err on the side of caution."

Hank was sent off on the jump, now, to make everything secure, while Skipper Tom took his place on the bridge deck at starboard to watch the weather.

"I guess there'll be time, now, Hank, to rig life lines on the bridge deck," hinted Halstead, coolly. "Never mind about any aft. Whoever goes below can go through the motor room."

Catching a look full of meaning in the young commander's eye, Butts hustled about his new task.

"You seem to be making very serious preparations," suggested Powell Seaton, seriously.

"Nothing like being a fool on the wise side," answered Skipper Tom, calmly.

Within ten minutes more the wind had freshened a good deal, and the "Restless" was bending over considerably to port, running well, indeed, considering her very small spread of canvas.

Now, the sky became darker. The weather was like that on shore in autumn when the birds are seen scurrying to cover just before the storm breaks.

"I reckon there's going to be something close to trouble, after all," observed Powell Seaton, when it became necessary for him to hold his hat on.

Tom nodded in a taciturn way, merely saying:

"If you're going to stay on deck, Mr. Seaton, you'd better put on a cap, or a sou'wester."

Mr. Seaton started below, through the motor room. While he was still there the gale struck, almost without further warning.

"Watch the wind and ease off a bit, Joe," bawled Skipper Halstead in his chum's ear.

Joe Dawson nodded slightly. The gale was now upon them with such fury that making one's self heard was something like work.

Despite the prompt easing by the helm, the "Restless" bowled over a good deal as the crest of the first in-rolling wave hit her.

Powell Seaton, a cap on his head, appeared at the motor room hatchway. Tom motioned him to remain where he was.

Clutching at the rail, Tom Halstead kept his face turned weatherward most of the time. He knew, now, that a fifty-five-foot boat like the "Restless," weather-staunch though she was, was going to have about all she could do in the sea that would be running in a few minutes more.

Nor did he make any mistake about that. A darkness that was almost inky settled down over them. Bending through the hatchway, the young sailing master yelled to Powell Seaton to switch on the running lights.

"For we'll need 'em mighty soon, if we don't now," Captain Tom added.

Hank reappeared with rain-coats, and with his own on. Hardly had those on deck so covered themselves when, accompanied by a vivid flash of lightning and a crashing peal of thunder, the rain came down upon them. At first there were a few big drops. Then, the gale increasing, the rain came in drenching sheets. The decks began to run water, almost choking the scuppers.

The heeling of the "Restless" was no longer especially noticeable. She was rolling and pitching in every direction, accompanied by a straining and creaking of timbers.

Powell Seaton, standing below, clutching for support, and not much of a sailor at best, began to feel decidedly scared.

"Are we going to be able to weather this, Captain Halstead?" he yelled up, as the young skipper paused close by the hatchway.

Though the noise of the now furious gale prevented Tom from making out the words very clearly, he knew, by instinct, almost, what had been asked of him.

"Weather the gale, sir?" Tom bawled down, hoarsely. "Of course! We've got to!"

There was a new sound that made the young sailing master jump, then quiver. With a great tearing and rending the single canvas gave way before the roaring gale. In a trice the sail was blown to fluttering ribbons!

CHAPTER XX
"C.Q.D! C.Q.D.!—HELP!"

"Lay along with me, Hank!" bawled the young skipper, hoarsely, in the steward's ear. "We've got to cut away what's left of the sail."

Neither helmsman could wisely be spared. Though the boat now had no power of her own she was being driven sharply before the gale, and some fine handling

83

of the wheel was needed in order to keep the boat so headed that she might wallow as little as possible in the trough of the sea.

Nor was the work of the young captain and Hank Butts anything like play. Making their way out along the top of the cabin deck-house was in itself hazardous. They were forced to clutch at any rigging that came to hand to avoid being washed overboard, for the waves were dashing furiously over the helpless boat.

It was not much of a task to haul in the sheet, making fast. Then, using their sailor's knives, they slashed away.

It was needful for one of them to go aloft.

"I can do it," proposed Hank, summoning all his courage.

"I know you can," Tom bawled in his ear. "But I'm not going to send anyone where I wouldn't go myself. It's mine to go aloft."

Thrusting his knife securely into the sheath at the end of its lanyard, Tom Halstead began to climb. Hank watched him closely. The pair at the wheel had no time to observe. All their attention was needed on their own work.

As he climbed, Tom Halstead had a sensation of being in danger of being pitched overboard.

Next, as the "Restless" lay over harder than she had yet done, it seemed as though the mast were bent on touching the water. Halstead had to halt in his climbing, satisfied to hold on for dear life.

"Oh, if we only had enough gasoline aboard!" groaned the young skipper, regretfully. "It would be a tough storm, even then, though nothing like as bad as this!"

As the boat partially righted herself, he went on with his climbing. At length he found himself where he could bring his knife into play, slashing away the fragments of the wind-torn canvas. When the work was done Halstead let himself to the deck again, half-expecting that the force of the pitching and fury of the gale would catch him and sweep him over into the dark, raging waters.

Yet he reached the deck in safety, finding himself beside Hank Butts, who, by this time, looked more like some water-logged thing than a natty steward.

"Come on below to the sail-locker," roared Captain Tom in the other boy's ear. "Be careful to hold to the life lines and go slow when the boat heels over. We'll get the new sail out and rig it—if we can."

Hepton, seeing them coming, made a sign to Joe, who stood doggedly braced at the wheel. Joe did all he could—it was little enough—to swing the boat's head a trifle so that she would ride more easily, if possible, in that terrible sea.

Slowly Tom and Hank made their way to the motor room door and slipped down below. There Powell Seaton, his face white, confronted them.

"Captain, this is awful. I don't see how the 'Restless' rides such a sea at all."

"She'd not only ride but steer well, sir, if we had gasoline enough to run her by her propellers," Halstead shouted back. "I'd go all the way to Havana in a gale like this if I could use the twin propellers. The 'Restless' is a sea boat, and she can't sink unless the watertight compartments are smashed."

"But she can turn over and ride keel upward, can't she?" demanded Mr. Seaton, with a ghastly grin.

"She can, sir, if she heels enough," Tom admitted. "But that's why Joe's at the wheel—because we need a fellow who can make the most out of such headway as the force of wind and waves gives us. And now, sir, Hank and I must try to rig a new sail."

Out of the sail-locker they dragged the new canvas. It was all in readiness for rigging. In calm weather they could have done this readily—but now? Only time could tell.

"Lend 'em a hand, Hepton!" roared Joe, as he saw the young captain and helper appear with the bulky canvas.

It was all the three of them could do, in the rolling, high seas in which the "Restless" pitched like a chip of wood, to get that sail on top of the cabin deck-house. Bit by bit they rigged it in place, working fast, straining muscle and sinew to hold the sail against the gale that strove to carry the canvas overboard. At last, they had it in place, ready for hoisting.

"Stand by to hoist," sang out Captain Tom. "The two of you. Go slow! I'll watch for trouble as you shake it out."

All the reefs had been taken in the sail before hoisting. Tom Halstead had made up his mind to be satisfied with just a showing of canvas to catch the high wind—enough to keep the boat steady.

As the sail went up, flapping wildly in the breeze, Halstead began to have his doubts whether it would last long. It was their last chance, however, for the control of the "Restless."

"Lay along here!" roared Tom, through his hands as a trumpet, when he saw that they had made the halyards fast. Now he signed to them to help him haul in on the sheet. Joe, watching, just making out the white of the canvas through the darkness, threw the wheel over to make the craft catch the wind. In a few moments more the gale was tugging against the small spread of canvas, and the "Restless" was once more under control—while the sail lasted!

All but exhausted, the trio found their way forward. For a brief space they tumbled below into the motor room, though Halstead stood where he could see Joe Dawson and spring to his aid when needed.

"Hank," called Halstead, five minutes later, "your trick and mine on deck. We'll give Joe and Hepton a chance to get their wind below."

Small as was the spread of canvas, Tom found, when he took the wheel, that the good little "Restless" was plunging stiffly along on her course. She was a wonderfully staunch little boat. The young sailing master bewailed his luck in having hardly any gasoline on board. It should never happen again, he promised himself.

Again? Was there to be any "again"? The motor boat captain was by no means blind to the fact that the "Restless" hadn't quite an even chance of weathering this stiff gale. At any moment the sail might go by the board in ribbons, as the first had done. Hank was not even watching the sail. If it gave way it must.

Joe presently came on deck for his next trick at the wheel. Hepton was with him.

"I've been thinking about the prisoner in the starboard stateroom," announced Joe. "It's inhuman to leave him there, locked in and handcuffed, in such a gale. He must be enduring fearful torment."

"Yes," nodded Tom. "I've just been thinking that I must go down and set him free as soon as I'm relieved."

"Go along, then," proposed young Dawson. "I have the wheel, and Hepton by me."

Taking Hank Butts with him, Tom Halstead made his way below.

"Dawson was just speaking to me about our prisoner," began Powell Seaton. "Dawson thinks he ought to be turned loose—at least while this gale lasts."

"Yes," nodded Captain Halstead. "I'm on my way to do it now."

"Will it be safe?"

"We can't help whether it is, or not," Skipper Tom rejoined. "It's a humane thing to do, and we'll have to do it."

Powell Seaton did not interpose any further objections. It would have been of little moment if he had, for, on the high seas, the ship's commander is the sole judge of what is to be done.

Even below decks, going through the electric-lighted passage and cabin, Tom and Hank made their way with not a little difficulty. They paused, at last, before the starboard stateroom door, and Tom fitted the key in the lock.

Jasper, the man locked within, faced them with affrighted gaze.

"We're going to the bottom?" he demanded, hoarsely, tremulously. His very evident terror gave the young skipper a new idea.

"Are you prepared to go to the bottom, Jasper?" demanded Halstead.

"Am I fit to die, do you mean?" asked the man, with a strange, sickly grin. "No, sir; I'm not. At least, not until I've cleared myself by telling a few truths."

"Come out into the cabin, man," ordered Halstead, leading him. "Now, sit down, and I'll get your handcuffs off."

The young captain of the "Restless" unlocked the irons about the fellow's wrists. Jasper stretched his hands, flexing his wrists.

"Now, I can swim, anyway, though I don't believe it will do much good," he declared.

"No; it won't do much good," Halstead assented. "We're something more than forty miles off the coast. But what do you want to say? What's on your mind? Be quick, man, for we must be on deck again in a jiffy. I don't want to lose my boat while I'm below with a rascal like you."

"I haven't always been a rascal," retorted Jasper, hanging his head. "At least, I have been fairly straight, until the other day."

"What have you been doing for Dalton and Lemly?" demanded Tom Halstead, fixing his gaze sternly on the frightened fellow.

"Never anything for Dalton," whined Jasper.

"Well, for Lemly, then?"

"Oh, I've been snooping about a bit, for two years or so, getting tips for Dave Lemly."

"What has Lemly been smuggling in the 'Black Betty' all this time?"

"Diamonds," admitted Jasper, sullenly.

Tom Halstead felt like giving a great start, but controlled himself.

"Smuggling diamonds under Anson Dalton's orders, eh?" insisted the young skipper.

"Yes; I reckon so."

"How did you come into our matter—as a guard and a traitor?"

"I was on hand when Mr. Seaton was getting his guards together," replied Jasper. "So was Dave Lemly's mate. The mate told me to jump in and get my chance with the guard."

"What other orders did you have?"

"I was to watch my chance to do anything nasty that I could," confessed the fellow, hanging his head.

"That was why you tried to ruin our aerials?"

"Yes."

"You also listened to Mr. Seaton and myself, the night we were going over to Lonely Island?"

Jasper squirmed, his face growing more ashen.

"You heard what was said about papers hidden in a cupboard at the bungalow. Did you? Answer me, confound you!"

With an appearance of utter rage Tom bounded at the fellow, as though about to attack him. Hank closed in, to be ready in case the attack turned out to be a genuine one.

"Yes, I stole an envelope full of papers," admitted Jasper.

"What did you do with them?"

"I turned them over to Dave Lemly."

"Where? On Lonely Island?"

"Yes; Lemly visited the island twice, at night, while I was on duty there," confessed the fellow, whining and letting his head fall lower.

"What else have you done against us?"

"Nothing, except trying to disable your wireless."

"Are you telling the whole, full truth?" demanded Captain Tom Halstead, surveying the fellow suspiciously. "As much of the truth as you want to lay bare before going to the bottom in this wild storm?"

"Yes! Oh, yes, yes!" insisted Jasper, easily. "Now, I've cleared my conscience of its load!"

"Humph!" muttered Tom Halstead, dryly.

At that moment a snapping sound overhead reached their ears. The "Restless" veered about, then heeled dangerously.

"Our second and last sail has gone!" cried the young skipper, starting forward. "Jasper, I hope you have told me the whole truth, for there is no knowing, now, how soon you'll start for the bottom—how soon we'll all go down. Helpless in this sea, the 'Restless' may 'turn turtle.'"

Nor was Tom speaking in jest, nor in any effort to scare the recent prisoner into a fuller confession. Indeed, the motor boat captain was paying no further heed to the wretch, but making his way forward. Jasper started to follow, Hank bringing up the rear.

As they reached the motor room the pitching and rolling of the boat were awesome enough. It seemed incredible that a boat the size of the "Restless" could live even a minute in her now helpless condition.

Joe still stood at the wheel, white-faced but calm.

"I don't see what we can do now, Tom," he shouted.

"Nothing but get down to the wireless, and do anything you can in the way of picking up some steamship," Halstead answered. "We might get a tow, or, at least, another spread of canvas for a third try to ride out the gale. The chances aren't big for us, but—well, Joe, we're sailors, and can take our medicine."

Joe smiled grittily as he edged away from the wheel after his chum had taken it.

"At least, if we go down, we go down in command of our own ship!" he yelled bravely in Tom's ear through the wild racket of the gale.

Then Joe went below. The storage batteries held electricity enough to operate the few lights and keep the wireless going at intervals for some hours yet.

Once, in the minutes that dragged by, Hank Butts thought of the fine spread he had been instructed to serve all hands that night. But no one else was thinking of food now. Coffee would have been more to the purpose, but to start a galley fire was to take the risk of adding fire at sea to the already more than sufficient perils of those aboard the "Restless."

Every few minutes Captain Tom Halstead called down through the speaking tube that connected him with Joe Dawson at the sending table. Always Joe's calm answer came, the same:

"Our wireless spark hasn't picked up any other ship yet."

Then, just as frequently, Joe would rest his hand on the sending key again, and send crashing off into space the signal:

"C.Q.D.!" The three letters that carry always the same message of despair across the waves.

"C.Q.D.!"—the wireless signal of distress. "Help wanted, or we perish!"

CHAPTER XXI
THE SPARK FINDS A FRIEND THROUGH THE GALE

The time had dragged on far into the night. Joe was still at the wireless sending table, sleepless, patient, brave—a sailor born and bred.

Jasper, like many another rascal a superstitious coward in the face of impending death, was seeking to appease the sting of his conscience by doing everything in his power to make amends in these grave moments. He stood by, pallid-faced yet collected enough to obey any order instantly.

Captain Tom remained on deck all the time now, though Hank often relieved him briefly at the wheel. Both Hepton and Jasper stood by to help as deck-hands. Powell Seaton came up on deck occasionally, though he remained more in the motor room.

Again and again Joe signaled—always that desperately appealing "C.Q.D.!" It was all the signal he needed to send out. Wherever heard, on land or water, the first operator to catch it would break in at once with a demand for further particulars.

Yet Joe's soul grew sick within him as time passed, and no such break came through the storm-laden air. For Dawson, as well as had he stood on deck, knew that this endless, malignant fury of the gale must sooner or later start the seams of the staunch little craft. Or else, struck by a wave bigger than any others, she would lie so far over on her beam ends that she must finish the manœuvre by "turning turtle"—lying with her keel uppermost, and the crew penned underneath to drown in haste.

"Nothing to report yet, Joe, old fellow?" came down Captain Tom's brave though anxious voice for perhaps the fortieth time.

"No reply to our signals, Tom," went back the answer.

"Do you think our spark is still strong enough to carry far?"

"Plenty of electric 'juice' left," Joe responded. "The spark is as strong as ever. Oh, if we only had as much gasoline!"

"Oh, if we only had!"

But ten minutes after that last call Joe again sent forth:

"C.Q.D.! C.Q.D.!"

Then down the receivers traveled a click—not loud, yet unmistakable.

"Where are you? Answer!" came the response, out of the air from some quarter.

In frantic haste Joe Dawson fell upon his key once more.

> Motor yacht "Restless!" Under no power whatever. Gasoline almost gone—saving the last for any emergency chance that comes to us. All canvas blown overboard. Do you get this?

It seemed to frenzied Joe Dawson as though many minutes passed, yet the response came promptly:

> Give us your present position, "Restless," as best you know it!

Joe obeyed with fingers that seemed themselves to be worked by electricity. The receiver of the message repeated Joe's response, to make sure that it was correct.

"Who are you?" Joe now broke in to answer.

> Havana liner, bound north, and, we believe, within thirty miles of you. Have you been signaling long?

"Seems as though I had been signaling for years," sent back Joe, laughing nervously to himself. The answer came:

> We'd heard you before, then, but there was a little mishap to our installation. You keep at your table to send and receive. I'll do the same at my end. Keep up your courage until we reach you. Be ready to burn Coston lights when we ask you to.

Then how fast Joe Dawson managed to talk up through the speaking tube! Tom Halstead, after first announcing the great news to the deck with a wild cheer, put Hank at the wheel and hurried below. Shortly, however, the young skipper was back on deck, bearing the wonderful news.

In smooth weather the Havana liner, ordinarily a fifteen-knot boat, would have reached them in two hours. Under the weather conditions of this wild night it was much later when the two craft were within hailing distance by signal lights. Hank was now in command of the deck, Skipper Tom and Powell Seaton being with Joe.

"Shall we try to send you a line for a tow?" came the demand from the liner.

"Yes," replied Halstead. Then, with a grimace he added:

"But the salvage charge for such a tow will call for more than we can raise, Joe, old fellow. I reckon the 'Restless' will have to be put up for sale to pay her own bills."

"Do you think I'd let you boys stand the towing charges?" demanded Powell Seaton, indignantly. "Whatever charges there are are mine to pay, and I'm at least good for the entire purchase price of a few boats like even this good little old salt water wizard!"

Tom soon afterwards made his way to the deck, but Mr. Seaton, weak and almost ill after the hours of anxiety, threw himself upon a cushioned seat near the wireless sending table.

As Tom stood on the bridge deck he studied the liner's lights as that larger craft manœuvred in to the leeward of the motor craft.

Once she had gained this position at a sufficient distance to make any collision on this wild sea unlikely, the liner steamed ahead.

"Stand ready to receive our line!" came to Joe in clicks through the watch-case receivers over either ear. He swiftly transmitted the order through the speaking tube to Halstead on the bridge.

Then the liner burned another light. Tom answered with one held in his own hand. It was the signal to look for the line, and the answer.

Through the darkness came a sudden, red flash from the after deck of the liner. The wind was so heavy that those on the bridge deck of the "Restless" could not be sure that they heard the report of the gun. But a missile whizzed over their heads, and to this blessed projectile trailed a thin line that fell across the top of the cabin deck.

Tom and Hank made a simultaneous bolt to get hold of that line. It was young Butts who secured it. He passed it on to the young captain, and, together, they leaped to the bridge-deck with it. From there they crawled forward over the raised deck, slipping the line, at last, between the two raised ends of the towing bitt.

"Now, haul in with a will," glowed the young skipper, as they crept back to the bridge-deck. A great wave swept over them on their way back. Tom saw it coming, and braced himself. Hank was caught by the rush of waters; he would have been swept overboard, but Halstead grabbed at one of his ankles, holding on grimly.

At that moment the late prisoner, Jasper, saw what was happening. Projecting himself forward over the raised deck, he, too, caught hold of Hank Butts, while Powell Seaton held to Jasper.

It was a sort of human chain by which Hank was pulled to safety. Tom, throughout the excitement, held the "thin line" in one hand.

"Haul in this thin line, quickly," shouted the young commander, who could barely make himself heard above the tumult of the gale.

As the line was some four hundred feet long, it used up precious moments to haul it and coil up the slack. As the last of the "thin line" came into their hands there came with it the first of a stouter hawser, the two lines being knotted securely together.

"Hold on to me, now! Form a chain again," ordered Skipper Tom. "I'll make the hawser fast forward."

All this while the Havana liner, some four hundred feet away, was going through a complicated bit of manœuvering under the hands of her officers. Alternately she moved at half-speed-ahead, at stop, or on the reverse, in order that, despite the high-rolling waves, she might not go too far ahead and snap the thin line. But now young Halstead soon had a stout hitch about the towing bitt at the bow. A few more turns, then he signaled to those behind holding him to help him back to the bridge deck. A dozen great waves had rolled over him on that smooth raised deck, but the members of the human chain hauled him back to safety.

"Signal to our friends that they can apply full speed ahead, Joe, if they want to," directed the young motor boat captain, briefly, as he reached the comparative safety of the bridge deck once more.

Over the noise of the gale the answering blast from the liner's whistle came to them as a far-away sound. But now the big boat ahead started on at a ten-knot speed.

"Gracious, but this seems good, once more!" glowed Tom Halstead, taking over the wheel as the towing hawser tautened and the "Restless" began to move forward under a headway that could be controlled and directed.

"We couldn't have stood this racket much longer, without a tow," chattered Joe. "I've had moments at the wheel, to-night, when, on account of our helplessness, I've felt sure we were going to 'turn turtle.'"

"What ails your jaws, old fellow?" demanded Tom, looking curiously at his chum. "Say, you're shaking to pieces, and I don't wonder. Get below and get dry and warm. Get below all of you, except one to stand by me. Who can best remain on deck for a few minutes more?"

"I can," proposed Jasper, starting forward with an odd mixture of sullenness and eagerness in his tone.

"I'll trust you—now," nodded Captain Halstead, after eyeing the man keenly. "The rest of you get below. We want a few dry folks aboard."

On board there was clothing in abundance, enough to enable everyone to make at least a few changes. Now that the "Restless" could be held to a course, Hank Butts cautiously made a small fire in the galley stove, and then stood by to watch the fire. After a while he had coffee going—this with a "cold bite" of food.

Hepton came up, bye-and-bye, to take the wheel. As he was wholly capable, Tom surrendered the helm to him, then dropped down below for some of that coffee.

"We've found out to-night what a wireless is good for," declared Joe. "But for it, we wouldn't have kept the 'Restless' afloat and right side up through the night."

"Until we got this tow I didn't expect ever to see port again," Tom Halstead admitted, quietly. "Do you know, the worst thing folks will have against row-boats in the future will be the fact that row-boats are too small to carry a wireless installation!"

"You feel wholly safe, now, do you, captain?" demanded Powell Seaton. "It rather seems to me that the gale has been getting heavier."

"It has," Halstead admitted. "If we were adrift, now, we probably couldn't keep right-side up for ten minutes. But give the 'Restless' real headway, and she'll weather any gale that a liner or a warship will."

"If the towing hawser should part!" shuddered Mr. Seaton.

"We'd hope to get another line across, and made fast, before we 'turned turtle,'" replied Skipper Tom.

No one could venture from below on the bridge deck without being quickly drenched. For that reason the wheel-reliefs were short. Hank, by staying right by his galley fire, was able to keep heat at which anyone coming down from the bridge deck could dry himself.

By daylight the gale and sea were lighter. For one thing, the Havana liner had carried her tow so far north that they were out of the worst of it. Half an hour after daylight the wireless operator aboard the larger craft telegraphed Joe:

"We've taken you in four miles off the town of Mocalee. You can get gasoline there. Do you want to cast off our line now?"

"Yes," flashed back Joe, after consulting Captain Halstead. "And our greatest, heartiest thanks for your fine work for us."

There was further interchange of courtesies, then the line was cast off as soon as Joe and Hank had started the twin motors going on the little that was left of the gasoline. There was no way, or need, to settle the liner's towing charges now. These could be collected later, for the "Restless" was a boat registered by the United States authorities. She could be found and libeled anywhere if her young owners failed to settle.

"Hooray! But doesn't it feel great to be moving under one's own power again!" chortled Captain Tom, as he felt the vibration of the propellers and swung the steering wheel.

Though the coast had been visible from daylight, the town of Mocalee was not in sight until the boat neared the mouth of a river. Up this stream, half a mile, nestled a quaint little Florida town, where, as one of the natives afterwards expressed it to Joe, "we live on fish in summer and sick Yankees in winter."

"We'd better get on shore, all hands, and stretch our legs," proposed Powell Seaton, after Skipper Tom had made the "Restless" fast at the one sizable dock of the town. "I see a hotel over yonder. I invite you all to be my guests at breakfast—on a floor that won't rock!"

"I'll stay aboard, then, to look after the boat," volunteered Hepton. "And you can rely on me to keep a mighty sharp eye on that man, Jasper," he added, in Halstead's ear.

It was after seven o'clock in the morning when the shore party from the "Restless," after strolling about a little, turned toward the hotel.

As they passed through a corridor on the way to the office Tom Halstead glanced at a red leather bag that was being brought downstairs by a negro bell-boy.

"Do you see the bag that servant has?" asked Tom, in a whisper, as he clutched Powell Seaton's arm. "Scar on the side, and all, I'd know that bag anywhere. It's the one Anson Dalton brought over the side when he boarded the 'Restless' from the 'Constant'!"

CHAPTER XXII
TOM HALSTEAD SPRINGS THE CLIMAX

"Can that fellow be here?" demanded Powell Seaton, his lips twitching.

"He must be—or else he has sent someone else with his baggage," Tom Halstead answered, in an undertone.

None of the party had paused, but had passed on into the office.

"We've got to know," whispered Powell Seaton, tremulously.

"Then you go ahead, sir, and register us for breakfast, and I'll attend to finding out about this new puzzle."

While Mr. Seaton went toward the desk, Tom signed to Hank Butts to follow him aside.

"About all you can do, Hank, is to get outside, not far from the door, and see whether Dalton goes out," Halstead declared, after having briefly explained the situation. "If Dalton leaves the hotel, give us word at once."

"Here, you take charge of this bag of mine, then," begged Hank, turning so that the clerk at the desk could not see.

Butts had come ashore in a long rain-coat drawn on over his other clothing. Now, he quickly opened a small satchel that he had also brought with him.

"That old hitching weight of yours!" cried Tom, in a gasping undertone, as he saw Hank slip that heavy iron object from the bag to a hiding place under his coat. "How on earth do you happen to have that thing with you?"

"It must have been a private tip from the skies," grinned Hank, "but I saw the thing lying in the motor room and I picked it up and slipped it into this satchel. Take the bag from me and I'll get out on the porch."

All this took place so quietly that the clerk at the desk noticed nothing. Halstead now carried the empty bag as he sauntered back to the party. But he found chance to whisper to Joe:

"Anson Dalton must be in this hotel. Hank is slipping out to watch the front of the house. Hadn't you better get around to the rear? If it happens that the fellow is about to leave here, it might be worth our while to know where he goes."

Nodding, Joe quietly slipped away. The negro with the red bag had now entered the office. The bag, however, he took over to the coat-room and left it there.

"Breakfast will be ready at any time after eight o'clock, gentlemen," announced the clerk.

Powell Seaton lighted a cigar, remaining standing by the desk. Tom stood close by. The door of the office opened. Anson Dalton, puffing at a cigarette, his gaze resting on the floor, entered. He was some ten feet into the room before he looked up, to encounter the steady gaze of Captain Halstead and the charter-man.

Starting ever so little, paling just a bit, Dalton returned that steady regard for a few seconds, then looked away with affected carelessness.

"Going to leave us to-day, Mr. Dalton?" inquired the clerk.

"I don't know," replied the scoundrel, almost sulkily. Then, lighting a fresh cigarette, he strolled over by one of the windows. Presently, without looking backward at the captain and charter-man of the "Restless," the fellow opened a door and stepped out onto the porch. There he promptly recognized Hank Butts, who stared back at him with interest.

"I wonder if Lemly is with this fellow?" whispered Halstead to his employer.

"I'm going beyond that, and wondering what the whole fact of Dalton's presence here can possibly mean," replied Powell Seaton.

The office door from the corridor opened again. Through the doorway and across the office floor stepped, with half-mincing gait, a young, fair-haired man who, very plainly, had devoted much attention to his attire.

"Where is Mr. Dalton?" demanded this immaculate youth, in a soft, rather effeminate voice that made Halstead regard him with a look of disfavor.

"You'll find him out on the porch, I think, Mr. Dawley," answered the clerk.

"Oh, thank you, I'm sure," replied the soft-voiced one. As though he were walking on eggs young Mr. Dawley turned, going toward the porch door.

"Oh, good morning, Dalton, dear fellow," cried the fair-haired dandy, in the same soft voice, as he came upon Seaton's enemy, who was walking up and down the porch utterly ignoring Hank Butts.

"Good morning, Dawley," replied Dalton, looking more than a little bored by the interruption.

"Now, who and what, in the game, is Dalton's Elizabeth-boy friend?" wondered Hank, eying the latest arrival.

"Have a cigarette, Dawley?" asked Dalton, in a voice almost of irritation, as he held out his case.

"Charming of you, indeed," declared Dawley, helping himself to a cigarette and lighting it.

"Look out the tobacco doesn't make you sick, babe," muttered Hank Butts under his breath.

"Now, my dear Dalton, about the business we were discussing here last evening—" began the soft-voiced one, but the other broke in on him with:

"If you don't mind, Dawley, I want to think a bit now."

"Oh, that will be quite all right, I am sure," agreed the soft-voiced one. "Then I'll just stroll down the street a bit and be back in time to breakfast with you."

Dalton nodded and the fair-haired fashion plate stepped down into the path and strolled away.

"All of which tells us," reflected Hank, "that our friend Dalton has been here at least since yesterday, and that he and the Elizabeth-boy dude are not very well acquainted."

Butts looked up, almost with a start, to find Dalton close at hand, scowling into the boy's face.

"I suppose you're out here to watch me," growled Dalton, glaring.

"If I am, you wouldn't expect me to grow confidential about it, would you?" asked Hank, grinning into the other's face.

"Oh, I don't want any of your impudence," snapped the rascal.

"I wouldn't give you any, or anything else belonging to me," clicked Hank Butts, decisively.

"If you're standing out here to watch me," continued Dalton, "I am willing to tell you that I am not leaving the hotel for the present."

"That, or any other information you are willing to offer me, will be treated in the utmost confidence, I assure you," promised Hank.

"Don't be too frolicsome with me!" warned Dalton, wrathily.

"I?" echoed Hank, looking astonished. "Why, I didn't say anything until you spoke to me."

With a snort Anson Dalton strolled away to a chair, seating himself and blowing out great clouds of smoke.

"He isn't exactly glad to see us here—I can guess that much," thought Hank. "But I wish I could guess how Anson Dalton comes to be here. I didn't see anything of his drab boat in the river."

In the meantime Tom Halstead and Powell Seaton, after dropping into chairs in the office, were talking most earnestly in undertones. From where they sat they could see Dalton's red bag resting on a shelf in the coat-room.

"I'd give the world to know whether the rascal has the stolen papers still in that bag!" cried Seaton, anxiously.

"Would he be likely to leave the bag around the hotel carelessly, if it contained anything so important?" asked Tom.

"He might have been willing to do so before he knew we were about here," replied the charter-man.

"But even when he knows we're here the fellow doesn't seem anxious about the matter."

"Because the clerk is behind the desk, where he can see everything," hinted Mr. Seaton.

"Yet, for all Dalton knows, the clerk might leave the room for a minute and give us our chance."

"I've an idea," muttered Mr. Seaton, rising so quickly that Tom stood up with him. "You keep the best eye possible over the rascal. Don't go in to breakfast unless he goes. Never mind whether I come to breakfast or not."

"All right, sir," nodded Halstead.

As Powell Seaton crossed the porch without even looking in Dalton's direction, the young motor boat captain also stepped outside, going over to Hank.

"Watch that fellow, Hank," whispered Tom. "Don't let him get away from you."

"Not if I have to steal his cigarettes," promised Butts, with vim.

Then Skipper Tom vanished, though not for long. He merely went to find Joe Dawson, at the opposite side of the building. The two chums returned together.

"Now," said Tom, in a chuckling whisper, "if Anse Dalton wants to get away from us, he'll have to run in four different directions at the same time."

"But did you see the nice plush boy that's with Dalton?" asked Hank, dryly. Butts, more than any of the others of the party, had taken a great dislike to the soft-voiced one.

Dalton turned, once in a while, to scowl in the direction of the three motor boat boys. That, however, was all the attention he gave them. A little later Dawley returned and seated himself beside his friend.

"Breakfast is ready, gentlemen," called the clerk, opening the door.

Not one of the Motor Boat Club boys stirred until after Dalton rose and stepped inside. Then they followed, close in the rear.

Dalton and his companion stepped into the dining room, installing themselves at a table not far from the door. Tom led the way for his party at the second table beyond. Two waiters appeared, one attending to each of the tables.

Dawley was evidently in bubbling spirits. He insisted on talking much, in his soft voice, to Anson Dalton, who was plainly annoyed. Tom Halstead glanced over at his enemy with an amused smile.

Yet no word passed between the tables. Food and coffee were brought, after some minutes, and at both tables the meal was disposed of slowly, excellent appetites being the rule.

Powell Seaton, in the meantime, had hastened to the telegraph office. From there he wired, "rush," to the chief of police at Beaufort, advising the latter that Anson Dalton was in Mocalee, and asking whether Dalton was wanted by the United States or state authorities on any charges growing out of the seizure of the schooner "Black Betty."

This dispatch sent off, Mr. Seaton, though remaining at the telegraph office, sent a messenger in haste for James Hunter, who represented Mocalee as chief of police and the entire police force.

"Jim Hunter," as he was locally called, a raw-boned, taciturn man, came speedily to the telegraph office. He was in his shirt-sleeves, chewing a straw, but he wore his police badge on his coat, while a short "billy" appeared in a hip pocket. Jim Hunter listened quietly while the operator, at Seaton's request, displayed the original of the telegram that had been sent to Beaufort.

Telegraph companies give quick service on telegrams relating to police business. So it was not long ere the operator's receiving instrument began to click with the local call.

The first dispatch that the operator passed out through the grated window was addressed to Powell Seaton, and signed by the chief at Beaufort. It read:

Thank you for information. Have wired chief of police, Mocalee.

The second telegram, following almost instantly, was addressed to the chief of police of Mocalee. It ran:

Arrest Anson Dalton, wanted by U. S. authorities on charge of
smuggling. Powell Seaton will point him out to you. Notify me
when arrested. Be careful to get all Dalton baggage. Hold for orders.

"That's all I wanter know," said Hunter, laconically, biting off the end of his straw and spitting it out. "Lead me to your friend Dalton, Mr. Seaton."

"I ought to warn you that he's a desperate fellow," murmured Mr. Seaton, as the pair left the telegraph office together.

"I've seen that kind before," nodded Mr. Hunter, curtly.

"Pardon me, but I notice you carry a club. Dalton will undoubtedly have a revolver, and he's likely to be ugly enough to attempt to use it," explained Mr. Seaton, apprehensively. "May I ask if you have a pistol, too?"

"I always carry all the tools I need," answered Jim Hunter. "I don't gen'rally 'low any man to pull a gun on me, though. Sometimes I'm quicker'n I gen'rally look."

There was an air of quiet, forceful reserve about this Florida policeman that made Powell Seaton feel more confident that the business in hand would not be defeated for lack of preparation. They made their way quickly to the hotel.

Anson Dalton and his soft-voiced companion were still at table, though evidently near the end of their meal.

Hank Butts, at a signal from his captain, had left the table. Hank had donned his rain-coat again, and was now waiting in the corridor leading to the stairs, in case Dalton should pass that way.

A moment later Joe left the table, stepping through the office and out onto the porch.

The Table Struck Hunter Amidships.

Dalton and Dawley were just rising when Halstead, seated where he could see out into the office, saw Seaton and a stranger enter.

"Now, the music will begin," thought Tom Halstead, throbbing.

"There he is, officer—the dark one!" cried Powell Seaton, leading the way into the dining room.

Jim Hunter lost no time. He made a spring in the direction of Anson Dalton, whose eyes flashed fire. Trained in a hard, desperate school, Dalton was fuller of tricks than the police chief had expected.

As Hunter rushed at him, Dalton forcefully pushed one of the small tables toward him. It struck Hunter amidships, most unexpectedly, and had the result of sending Mocalee's police force sprawling to the floor.

"You can't stop me—you shall not!" roared Anson Dalton. He made a dash for the doorway leading to the office. Swift as he was, Tom Halstead darted through ahead of him.

"He'll try to get that red bag—and he'll put up a fight with a pistol!" flashed through the young motor boat skipper's brain. "I'll fool him so far as the bag is concerned."

Diving into the coat-room, the door of which stood open, Halstead was in season to snatch up the bag. He turned, to find Dalton rushing at him, hands reached out.

Ducking under, Tom eluded Dalton, and darted across the office.

"Let some of the others catch him," gritted Halstead, inwardly. "What we want most to know may be in this bag!"

It was all done so quickly that Skipper Tom was across the office, pulling open the door into the corridor, before Anson Dalton bounded after him.

Joe Dawson rushed in from the porch, but too late to be of immediate help. Officer Hunter had sprawled badly, and Mr. Seaton had halted to aid him to his feet.

"Drop that bag, or you'll wish you had—no time for this nonsense," blazed Dalton, angrily, thrusting his right hand at his hip pocket.

CHAPTER XXIII
HANK BECOMES REALLY TERRIBLE

Bump! Whack!

Tom Halstead tried to slam the door shut in his pursuer's face, but one of Dalton's feet barred the closing, then thrust the door open.

As Halstead raced into the corridor Anson Dalton was close behind him, his hand yanking a revolver from his pocket.

There would have been a shot in another instant. Halstead might have been badly hit.

But Hank Butts, on duty in the corridor, had heard the cries.

As the door was thrust open Hank leaped forward. Out from under his rain coat he brought that same old hitching weight.

There was an instant, only, for action, but young Butts was an expert with the weapon he had made his own.

His hands flew aloft, then descended, just as Anson Dalton's left foot was thrust forward in his running.

"Halt, you—" roared Dalton.

Bim! Down came the hitching weight, and landed squarely across the left foot of the pursuer. Dalton let out a fearful yell, while his revolver fell to the floor. There was a flash and a crashing explosion in that confined space; the weapon had been harmlessly discharged.

As for Dalton, he swayed dizzily for a few seconds, trying to lift the injured foot. Then, with a groan and a burst of ugly language, he sank to the floor.

Hank darted in, securing his hitching weight and backing off with it once more.

Though he had heard the discharge of the pistol, Jim Hunter did not stop to reach for his own revolver. He leaped through into the corridor, his pocket police club in hand.

"There he is, but you won't have to club him any," announced Hank, dryly, pointing to the groaning Dalton. "He'll eat out of your hand, now—will Anson Dalton."

Pausing only to drop his club to the floor, Jim Hunter whipped out a pair of handcuffs from a cavernous pocket, bent over Dalton, and—

Snap-click! The troublesome enemy of the motor boat boys was not only badly hurt, but a secure prisoner as well.

Now, Seaton and the boys gathered about the law's captive.

"I reckon you'll have to git up," announced Jim Hunter, putting a helping hand under one of Dalton's arms.

"I can't—oh, stop! Let up! My foot's crushed. I can't stand on it!" yelled Dalton.

Hunter came quickly to realize the fact that Dalton could not stand with much comfort. Joe came up with a chair, onto which the prisoner was allowed to sink.

"Oh, you boys think you've finished things for me, don't you?" leered Dalton, glaring around him in a rage. "But you haven't. You'll soon find that you've just begun to stir up trouble for yourselves."

"Go easy, man—do!" begged Hunter, soothingly. "Of course yer pet corn feels bad just now. But, say! That's the niftiest way of stopping a bad man, I reckon, thet was ever invented."

"Is it?" groaned Dalton. Then, catching the trace of a smirk in Hank's eyes, the rascal shook his fist at the steward of the "Restless," snarling:

"I'll find my own way to settle with you!"

"Take your time—when you're feeling better," Hank begged, cheerfully.

Fair-haired, soft-voiced young Dawley had followed the crowd out into the corridor. The hotel clerk, the proprietor and three or four of the servants all had increased the crowd there. Dawley rapidly learned what had happened.

"It's a beastly outrage," he announced, his soft voice sounding almost harsh in the indignation that he felt.

"Oh, take a fan, Dolly, and go out on the porch to cool off," growled Joe Dawson.

One of the servants, in the excess of excitement, actually took the fair-haired youth by the shoulders, and, though the latter protested, thrust him out through the open door onto the porch, slamming the door after him.

"That's too bad," grinned Hank. "I'll go out and see if the poor fellow has fainted."

As Butts stepped out on the porch, closing the door shut after him, Dawley, his cheeks very red, leaped out from the chair into which he had sunk.

"It was you who played that mean trick on my friend," cried Dawley, in a voice which he fondly believed trembled with rage.

"Yes," admitted Hank, meekly.

100

"I'll punish you for that!" quivered the soft-voiced one, stepping forward.

"Don't strike me on the wrist," pleaded Hank. "I have rheumatism there."

But Dawley, too angry, or else too dull to understand that he was being made a mark for ridicule, continued to advance upon Butts, who retreated, a look of mock alarm in his face.

"Keep away from me—please do, while you're angry," begged Hank, still retreating.

"I won't!" snapped Dawley. As Hank now retreated rapidly backward, Dawley went after him with corresponding speed.

"If you must have it, then, why—take it!" cried Hank, in a tone of desperation.

One of his hands had been held under his rain-coat all along. Now Hank thrust the other hand inside, as well, to reach for some object concealed there.

"Oh. O-o-oh! Don't you drop that weight on my foot!" yelled Dawley, blanching and falling up against the wooden wall.

But Hank, ruthlessly, as one whose blood is up, brought both his hands swiftly into view as he sprang at Dawley. There was a yell from the fair-haired one as Hank bent forward, then dropped squarely on the toes of Dawley's right foot— his *pocket-handkerchief*!

"There, now!" mimicked Hank Butts, turning on his heel.

A roar of laughter came from Mr. Seaton, Tom, Joe and two or three of the bystanders who had followed outside.

CHAPTER XXIV
CONCLUSION

"I'm sorry, young man," said Powell Seaton, resting a hand on Dawley's collar, "but the chief of police wants to see you."

"I'm not arrested, am I?" demanded the soft-voiced one, in a tone of great alarm.

"I think not. But come along. The chief wants to see you in the office."

There they found Hunter and his manacled prisoner, who had been carried into the office just as he sat on the chair.

"Where's that red bag that started all the trouble?" demanded Chief Hunter. Joe Dawson produced it.

"You can't open that," leered Dalton, though he spoke uneasily.

"If we can't unlock it, we'll cut it open with a sharp breadknife," mocked Hunter. "Yet I reckon thet we'll find the key in yer pocket."

This guess turned out to be correct. The key was inserted in the lock and the bag opened. Powell Seaton pushed forward to help the police official in the inspection of the contents.

"There are my papers," cried Powell Seaton, grabbing at two envelopes.

"Look 'em over, ef you want, but I reckon I'll haveter have 'em to go with the prisoner," assented Chief Hunter.

"They're the same papers that this fellow stole—one set from Clodis, and the other from my bungalow through a helper," cried Mr. Seaton.

Anson Dalton watched Seaton with a strange, sinister look.

"Gracious! Look at these, here!" gasped Chief Hunter, opening a small leather case. Nearly a score of flashing white stones greeted his eyes.

"Di'munds, I reckon," guessed the police chief.

"Yes; Brazilian diamonds," confirmed Powell Seaton. "Probably this prisoner's share or proceeds from smuggling in diamonds. That business, then, was what the 'Black Betty' was used for."

"Those are the diamonds I came down here to negotiate for," broke in Dawley, wonderingly.

"You?" demanded Hunter, surveying the soft-voiced one.

"Yes; my father is Dawley, the big jeweler at Jacksonville," explained the youth. "Here's his card. I'm the buyer for the house, and your prisoner wrote that he had some fine stones to sell."

"They're fine, all right, or I'm no judge of Brazilian diamonds," nodded Powell Seaton. "But I guess the United States Government owns them, now, as a confiscated prize."

A carriage was brought around to the door, and Anson Dalton was driven to the county jail, eight miles away, to be locked up there pending the arrival of United States officers.

Dawley easily proved his innocence, and the truth of his own story. Despite his effeminate manners and soft voice, it afterwards developed that the youth was a skilled buyer of precious stones, and a young man of no little importance in the business community of his home town.

Following the swift succession of events at the little Florida town, there came a lull in the long strain of excitement and danger.

Every now and then Dick Davis and Ab Perkins, aboard the Rio-bound "Glide," found a chance to have a wireless message relayed back to the United States.

These messages came in veiled language, according to instructions, but they conveyed to Powell Seaton the joyous news that these two far-away members of the Motor Boat Club were proceeding safely on their long journey, and that no harm was happening to them, nor to the precious papers in their care.

One fine day a cablegram came all the way from Rio Janeiro which told that Dick and Ab had reached that Brazilian city, and had turned over the papers in their care to the waiting American for whom they were intended.

A week after that came another cablegram, announcing that the American syndicate had succeeding in locating the lost diamond field, and that papers for a proper patent were being filed with the Brazilian Government.

Right on top of that came the news, in the daily press, that Governor Terrero, of Vahia, had been shot and killed by an escaped prisoner—a former enemy whom the governor had greatly and wickedly harassed.

Captain Dave Lemly was captured about this time. He and Dalton, it developed, had been the principal American agents in a big scheme for smuggling Brazilian diamonds into the United States. The gems, it was shown, were secretly shipped in quantities from Rio, aboard a sailing ship. This ship, carrying a general cargo, was always met near Beaufort by Lemly, in the "Black Betty," and the diamonds were taken on the little black schooner. As the "Black

Betty" sailed as a fishing boat, Dave Lemly had always been able to evade the American customs authorities, and a hugely profitable business in diamond smuggling had been built up.

Governor Terrero, of the state of Vahia, Brazil, it is supposed, was behind the southern end of the smuggling scheme, though this has not been proved. Dalton, acting as the governor's go-between and spy, had played his part well and desperately. Yet now, in the end, Dalton was convicted on the evidence furnished by some of the members of the late crew of the "Black Betty." So was Lemly, and both are now serving long sentences in prison, along with the members of the crew of the smuggling schooner.

Clodis recovered, after a few weeks. He was handsomely rewarded by the new diamond syndicate for the dangers through which he had run. He last remembered descending the stairs to the "Constant's" stairs, and had no recollection of having been struck down.

All the members of the guard over at Lonely Island were more than handsomely paid. Even Jasper was forgiven, and well rewarded.

After he had been in prison some length of time Anson Dalton one day confessed to Mr. Seaton's attorney that, while at sea on the drab boat (which was afterwards found and confiscated by the revenue people), he, Dalton, had copied the stolen papers, intending to send one set southward and retain the originals.

After losing both the "Restless" and the "Glide" in the fog, Dalton had had Lemly put in to shore. There they had been met by a trusted Brazilian spy for Governor Terrero. The Brazilian, with the copies of the papers, had hurried to New York by train. This Brazilian did not succeed in starting for Rio until some days after the "Glide" had sailed, and, moreover, he went on a slower boat. So, by the time the Brazilian spy arrived at Rio, the American syndicate had located the lost diamond field, had filed patents with the Government, and Terrero had died. So all of Anson Dalton's plotting had come to naught.

One of Powell Seaton's first acts was to adjust fully the claim of the Havana line for the towing of the "Restless" through that fearful northeast gale.

While waiting for the final news of the success of his plans, the charter-man cruised much up and down the coast with the boys of the "Restless." Then afterwards, through the month of November, Seaton enjoyed another cruise with them.

The charter money was not all that Captain Tom, Engineer Joe and Steward Hank received for their splendid work.

As soon as the final plans of the great new American diamond syndicate at Rio Janeiro had been established on a safe and firm basis, the charter-man of the "Restless" was prepared to talk of a splendid reward. His plans were so big, in fact, that all three of the boys felt bound to call a halt. Yet the reward that they *did* finally accept made very important additions to the bank accounts of all three of these daring young motor boat navigators.

Dick Davis and Ab Perkins, on their return from Rio, were "remembered" by Mr. Seaton with bank drafts the size of which almost took away their breath.

Then came a new cruise, a new set of adventures in new surroundings. It was a cruise which the many friends of our Motor Boat Club boys will agree was the most wonderful, the most exciting, and certainly the most mysterious lot of adventures through which any member of the Club ever passed. The details of what happened, however, must be reserved for the next volume in this series, which will be published under the title: "THE MOTOR BOAT CLUB IN FLORIDA; Or, Laying the Ghost of Alligator Swamp."

[THE END]

CPSIA information can be obtained at www.ICGtesting.com
Printed in the USA
LVOW06s1809130414

381513LV00023B/1252/P